GLASS MOUNTAIN

GLASS MOUNTAIN

CYNTHIA VOIGT

DIVERSIONBOOKS

Diversion Books
A Division of Diversion Publishing Corp.
443 Park Avenue South, Suite 1008
New York, New York 10016
www.DiversionBooks.com

For more information, email info@diversionbooks.com

First Diversion Books edition March 2017.
Print ISBN: 978-1-63576-111-5
eBook ISBN: 978-1-68230-160-9

1

VALENTINE'S DAY

We are none of us what we seem.

That was my thought as I stopped on the landing, a thought to which I quickly added, *Except for those of us who are exactly what we seem.* The mirror became a full-length portrait.

I looked just right—not too handsome. Realistically handsome, plausibly handsome, broad shoulders, good cheekbones, strong eyebrows—I looked like some dark, sleek animal, a panther, maybe a lynx, or tiger. Not one of those wispy zoo animals but a *National Geographic* photograph—the beast in his habitat. Rude good health, brute strength, caught on the prowl.

No matter how I moved, I couldn't bring the third staircase into the portrait. Degas might have brought all the background in by distorting the point of view, Rembrandt might have suggested it in the shadowy darkness behind the illuminated figure, but only Picasso in his cubist period could have painted the portrait truly.

I went on down.

In the kitchen I put the day's message onto the answering machine. "You have reached the Mondleigh residence," I spoke over the tiny grate. Who knows how these devices work? And until they don't work, who cares? "Please leave your name and telephone number, so that your call can be returned." I looked up at the calendar and added a personal touch, "A good Saint Valentine's Day to you."

The machine reset itself with a busy whirring sound and I played the message back, to be sure it had recorded properly, and to enjoy the sound of my voice. Everything was as it should be.

Taking up a scarf from the chair, I went back along the hall, punched in the alarm code, and stepped into the vestibule. The leaded glass door locked itself automatically behind me. I opened the wooden front door, pulled on my gloves, and stepped out into the sunlight.

At midday, even the city air was sweet with the promise of spring, spring coming, soon now. I could taste that promise behind the damp chill of winter and the perpetual New York fumes. It was there, spring's sweetness, like the perfume of a woman who has just left the room, the perfect woman and you may never meet her. But you know—as you walk into the room and catch the last, faint, already fading whiff of her presence—that if you do, she will enchant you. And have you for life. Like any sensible man, you are both terrified and eager.

I turned east, away from the park, then north along

Madison among the minks and poodles, the sports satchels and portfolios. I turned east again on Eighty-Seventh, across Park, across Lexington, down toward the river, to the Wilshire Gallery.

The Wilshire has taken its lesson from the Guggenheim—broad spaces where the walls flow as smoothly as the light from room to room, each painting isolated. I walked slowly around, as if I were considering the works seriously. This was a bridge-and-rooftop painter, a student of angles, whose palette ranged from muddy black to muddy white, with brief stopovers at muddy gray and muddy brown. The red signature—NEMO—beaconing out of every canvas, suggested a flawed sense of the place of the artist in society.

One painting halted me: a three-dimensional rectangle the color of muddy gold floated on a muddy green background. When I moved close to the canvas, I could make out thick shapes on the rectangle, as if letters had been stamped into it. A *K* or maybe it was an *R*, or both? Further on a *GE*, an *S* at the end, unless it was an *8*, but I thought I understood.

"You think it's a joke?"

I turned at the man's voice. He was in his late fifties, a pale fleshy face and shrewd eyes, a blue blazer over a blue turtleneck atop Royal Stewart trousers; his pinky ring glittered with a row of diamonds.

"If you don't mind my asking," he said.

"I don't mind," I said.

"What would you say, is it worth nine thousand dollars? I can't tell: is it a sound risk?"

"A sound risk?"

"They keep telling me, 'Invest in art, you can make a killing,' but I don't believe them, who can believe them? Property's what I know, and I know how that works. I look at a building, say—walk around in it, get the feel of it—and I *know*. You know? In my gut." He jabbed a finger at his stomach. "I'd be happier with gold. Wouldn't you?"

"Gold always appeals," I said.

"That's what I told 'em, the whole crew of them. 'Nobody ever lost his shirt in gold,' I said. And they sneak looks at one another as if I was crazy...and I'm the one with the money. I could buy and sell all of them and their business too, if I wanted. Which I don't. Experts, I ask you. What are you in? If you don't mind my asking."

I didn't mind. "This and that," I told him. "Stocks and bonds. Domestic services."

"Domestic services, is there money in that?"

"You'd be surprised."

"So you'd advise me not to buy this."

"I'm not advising anyone."

"Yeah, I hear you, but just answer me this. Are you going to be picking it up?"

I shook my head.

"I rest my case." He was pleased with himself, pleased with me. "I'm glad I ran into you, young fellow. You look like someone who knows what's what, that's my gut reaction. Those guys don't give me the same good feeling. But they can't run me in circles, I'll let them know that." He stepped up close to the picture, leaned his face into it. "Because this stuff is junk. I don't know anything about art, but I know garbage when I see it. If you don't mind my saying so."

He departed abruptly. I figured he was going off to blister his financial advisers, and they probably deserved it, if for no better reason than breaking the basic law of economy that states that the tune the piper plays is called by the man who pays. Or woman.

I took the broad staircase up to the second floor, following my own plans for the day. Mr. Plaid Pants had been a diversion, not a distraction.

I recognized her right away. She sat on a low bench, facing a canvas that splayed its angularity over half the long wall. She wore a broad-brimmed hat, and her tawny hair brushed at her shoulders. She was alone.

I didn't rush at her. I don't rush women. It's disrespectful to them, and to me too, as if the only way I could win a woman is by the emotional equivalent of a football tackle—knock her sideways, off balance, breathless, and down. As if the only way I could attract her is for my pheromones to grab her hormones by the throat and shake them into mindlessness, and then she will take me to herself. Which otherwise she wouldn't think of doing.

Slowly, I circled the room. She paid no attention to me. I wondered what she was thinking. Was she trying to picture the painting on a particular wall, immersing herself in a decorating dilemma? Did she see something in the canvas that made life palatable, comprehensible, endurable? Or did she see something that troubled her spirit and was she concentrating on capturing the idea before it was lost to her? Was she killing time while awaiting a friend, a lover, a husband, awaiting an appointment, or the time when she could have her next meal? Which is at least doing something, something to do. Or was she waiting for the chance of me?

Taking a seat on the bench, I kept my eyes on the painting, first, then turned for a brief look at her, an unaggressive look, unassuming, a stranger's glance at a nearby stranger. Her hair was entirely lovely. It seems to me possible to love a woman for the beauty of her hair.

"Strength and boldness," I said, my attention back on the picture. "It certainly has those. Are you thinking of buying it?"

We sat side by side, like the profiled emperor and his consort of a Byzantine coin.

"No." She shook her head and her hair swung like heavy cloth.

After a while she asked, "Are you?"

"No." Like her, I didn't say that I couldn't afford to hang twelve thousand dollars on my walls.

After another little quiet time, during which she sat without moving, she added, "I have two Nemos already."

I followed the pace she set and waited before I answered. "They may prove a good investment."

Then she did turn to look at me. "I don't buy art as an investment."

"Good," and I smiled entirely frankly. "Good for you." She had perfect teeth. "Maybe you can answer a question. The painter's name—what do you call it, a *nom de palette*? Do you know if it's the classical reference? Or the Victorian?"

"That, I won't tell you."

Not *can't, won't*. If not Homer or Verne, then what? I wondered; there was some secret she wanted me to know she was keeping. I asked her to lunch.

She hesitated, itself a compliment. She took a pair of leather gloves out of her purse and held them in her hands. "Are you married?" she asked.

This is a tricky question and when it gets asked early on it's hard to know how to respond. "Yes," I hazarded.

The wrong answer—although it might be that *no* would have been equally wrong. She might have chosen a question which, no matter how I answered, would become her reason to refuse me.

"I make it a rule never to go out with married men, not even for lunch." She rose, and I rose with her. She turned and went down the staircase. She knew I was watching: her head turned to one side and the other as she descended, so her hair could swing beautifully.

I sat down again, alone, waiting and thinking.

Three women in their early twenties chattered together as they came up the stairs. Over from First Avenue, I guessed, one a student, the others salesgirls in boutiques, and I would have guessed, if asked, that they were roommates. Nobody asked but I guessed anyway.

I didn't approach them, although the tallest looked queryingly at me. They were on a lunch-hour visit. The student wore a pair of wing-tipped shoes, which gave her legs a wonderfully gamine look; one salesgirl wore plain low heels, which emphasized her wonderfully slender ankles; and the other wore equally plain pumps with a higher heel, which emphasized the wonderful plumpness of her calves.

Women, I thought, are more at ease than men with

variety of style or with variety of manner, more at ease with variety. In literature and art, and especially in the mythology of the arts, the heroic man is a raging individualist, but perhaps it is his rarity that makes him heroic. Women, I think, are the natural anarchists.

I sat for an hour or more, but the only other woman to catch my eye—her emerald earrings swung in the light—was joined by a stout and prosperous overcoat whose fingers on her elbow left no doubt about who she was lunching with. She greeted him gladly and leaned forward for a welcoming kiss; her emeralds winked at me like conspiring little devils. When I was hungry enough, I descended the stairs to claim my coat. On impulse, I asked the gallery attendant if she was free for lunch. She considered me. "Are you married?"

"Why no," I hazarded.

"I'm sorry," she said, and seemed sincere. She held the heavy glass door open for me. "I make it a rule never to accept invitations from unmarried men."

2

I MEET HER

I was welcomed at the restaurant in the language particular to upscale New York waiters—part French, part Irish, with something of Italian liquidity to it, especially around the gestures—and seated without delay. I asked for a glass of the young Sangiovese and on the waiter's recommendation ordered veal; with everything settled, I sat back and looked around the room.

Besides myself, she was the only person eating alone. It's unusual to see a woman eating alone in such a restaurant, especially lunch, especially a young woman. A bright metal bucket was set beside her, the swathed bottle resting a little askew, the tulip glass half-filled with champagne. She seemed lost in contemplation of the glass and her hands. She looked barely old enough to be drinking legally, if she was in fact old enough.

There are millions of people in New York on any working day. Over half of them are women, and perhaps four percent of those have money of their own, and maybe ten percent of those—a tenth of that twenty-fifth of that half—are what might be called monied. I studied the solitary young woman.

She had a fresh-from-the-salon look, everything about her carefully in place, everything new and expensive. Because her head was bent, I couldn't see much of her face, just a part of a cheek, the chin line, half of a bright-red mouth, and the rest a long tumble of curls. The wild gypsy look, which women seem to like on themselves, was at odds with her baby-blue dress with its wide sailor-style white collar and long sleeves. The red lipstick matched the red piping on collar and cuffs, matched the red nail polish, matched the red boots visible under the tablecloth. She looked like a doll somebody had dressed up to go out with. I wondered if she had been stood up for a lunch date; she had a stood-up look to her. Her cheeks were pink, but whether from blusher, champagne, shame, or chagrin I had no way of knowing.

A plate was put in front of her and she toyed with her food but didn't eat much. Her glass was kept full. She kept emptying it. The bold nails were at odds with the hesitant movements of her ringless hands.

I didn't stare at her as openly as it sounds. I drank my wine, ate my own lunch, looked around the room, thought my thoughts. I was savoring my coffee when she asked for her bill. Her red purse looked unworn, stylish, too small to carry much more than comb, lipstick, powder, and a couple of credit cards.

I paid cash, as always, and tipped generously. I was in no hurry to leave, so I watched her carefully sign her receipt, carefully slide out from behind the table, and walk carefully to the door to the coatroom. It *was* a sailor dress she was wearing. Between the shapeless blouse, the full skirt, and the boots, her figure was effectively concealed. She was short, I could see that, but I doubted my own eye because in everything else—hair, makeup, dress, foot-wear—her appearance was designed for a tall woman, a tall and stylishly thin woman, most certainly a woman old in experience. This girl suggested innocence. But the coat she accepted was a long, dark, worldly mink, and she puzzled me.

Perhaps she had no mother. Perhaps her mother had bad taste, or kept herself young by keeping the daughter younger. Or perhaps this young woman was convinced that as long as she spent a lot of money, she was getting her money's worth.

I didn't follow her out of the restaurant. I wasn't that puzzled; she was only a girl. It was, however, not many minutes later that I stood outside the entrance, looking up and down the street, assuring the waiter that yes, my meal had been delicious, and yes, I had tried the veal, which had been all he had promised. The young woman in mink was, I noticed, making her slow way down the street.

While we watched, she wobbled over to a set of scrubbed steps and sat. A nanny wheeling her pram toward us made a wide circle around the hunched figure.

"She's never been in the restaurant before, not that I remember," the waiter said. "But I mean, look at her.

15

She's not a woman you'd remember." He had forgotten his accent.

After a brief rest, she pulled herself erect and hesitated. A man walking toward her looked at her, and she looked down at the ground before moving on her wobbly way. He gave her the kind of smile that explains why women have taken up martial arts and approached closer.

"What a city this is," the waiter remarked, accent remembered. "Terrible, yes?"

That would have been a long argument, so I just nodded my head as if I were agreeing and buttoned my coat. She had crossed to the opposite side of the street and the man had started to cross to intersect her but, seeing me, veered off by the time I overtook her.

I put a gloved hand on her arm—not the upper, intimate arm, but the lower arm, just above the wrist, and just the slightest of touches. I spoke in my plummiest voice. "Excuse me, miss?"

She stopped. Her quick glance had nothing but alarm in it. She wasn't a girl. She was old enough to be wary of chance encounters, and her face had none of the unfinished look of girlhood. "I'm sorry," she said, "I'm on my way…" She spoke with slow self-consciousness, and she swayed gently where she stood.

"You've had too much to drink," I said, nonjudgmental, impersonal.

She moved to pull her arm away but the gesture almost unbalanced her, so I held on. Fur is slippery, not easy to grip with gentlemanly firmness.

"I don't think I know you." She spoke almost in a whisper. "I'll scream for help." She looked carefully at me. "Do I know you?"

"I was in the restaurant. Let me get you a cab. Really, I'm safe." There was no reason for her to believe me.

She drew herself up. Even in the high-heeled boots she didn't reach my shoulder. "I don't want a cab. Thank you."

"You can't wander the streets like this."

"A cab would take me home."

"Home is the best place for you."

She shook her head, then reached out to steady herself on my arm. "I've had too much to drink," she said. "I need to sit down."

I raised my hand to signal an approaching cab. "That's right, you do. You're absolutely right. That's very sensible of you." The cab pulled up beside us, halting traffic. I opened the door for her. A few horns protested the inconvenience. She hesitated.

"I can't go home. You don't understand. It was fine when I was sitting down, I was fine."

I nudged her toward the interior. Surprise made her sit, her legs out of the cab, her purse on her lap. "Tell the man where to take you."

"No." Sullen, mulish refusal.

"It's not wise not to go home. Even this part of town isn't safe. You need to go home and sleep it off."

She pulled her legs into the cab—"You can't make me"—and slid across the seat to the opposite door.

I got in, again holding her by the mink, and pulled the door closed beyond her, and pulled the door closed behind me. Horns honked. "You want a cab or not?" the cabbie asked.

"No," she said.

"Yes," I told him.

She giggled. "But we haven't been introduced," and tears slid out of her eyes.

The cab inched closer to the parked cars, letting those from behind pass. One blared as it went by, to let us know we were not forgiven. "Where do you live?" I asked her.

"I can't go home," she wailed.

I could have shaken her.

"Mister," the driver reminded me.

"It was only champagne. I was only sitting down. I can't stand up."

"Look, mister, you're costing me money."

"I don't have to tell you." She wouldn't look at me. "Nobody can make me. Can they?"

The cabbie was easier to deal with, so I did that. "Just drive. Anywhere. To the park, take us to the Seventy-Second Street entrance."

He pulled out into the line of traffic. Horns greeted him.

"What are you doing?" She sounded frightened now.

"I'm taking you for a walk."

"I'll scream. Do you hear me? Driver, stop."

He pulled over, cars honked, and she reached for the door handle.

I held her wrist. "Be reasonable. You won't go home, wherever that is, you're drunk—"

"Am not."

I didn't laugh, but it was an effort.

"You can't get drunk on champagne," she told me.

I was tempted—I really was—to leave her to her own

devices. I think if she had looked drunk enough to throw up, I would have. But she didn't have that greeny-white, sweating look and I didn't have anything better to do with the afternoon, so I stuck with her. With it. My knight-in-shining-armor act.

"You need to walk it off. Or at least walk some of it off."

"Not sitting down you can't, not champagne. Everybody says. I know."

"And I'm probably the safest man in a ten-block radius."

At that she lifted her face. "Probably twenty," she said. "Maybe in all of Manhattan. I'm sorry, I should thank you."

"You're welcome," I said. "Drive on, cabbie."

He did, crossing an avenue. She smiled at me, without showing any teeth, all sweet reason. "I'm sitting down. Everything's all right now. I'm fine now. You can leave me alone. Cabs are safe places, they have to be: the drivers have to pass a test. What's his name?" she leaned forward to peer at his license. "Leonard. Leonard? Stop this cab at once. Please."

He obeyed her, grinning at me in the mirror. At least somebody was enjoying himself.

"Take us to the park, Leonard," I said, in my most commanding voice. "The Seventy-Second Street entrance."

He hesitated, thinking, then made up his mind and pulled out again. "I hope you're a big tipper, mister."

"But you can't, you can't do this. Listen, what's your name, Leonard? This man is a perfect stranger. I want to go home."

I seized on that. "And where would home be?"

"Uh-uh." She shook her head from side to side. "You're not going to trick me that way. You know I can't go home, not like this." She turned away from me to glare out the window.

We got out at the park, where I hoped the presence of many people would be reassuring to her. She marched along beside me quietly enough but plumped herself down on the first bench we came to, coat collar turned up, coat held around her, so that she looked like a giant, overfed mink. She wouldn't look at me. She didn't speak.

I didn't insist. I was only cooperative. When she got up and walked, I went with her. When she sat, I sat. We circled the pond, walking and sitting. It must have been a couple of hours. Finally, she turned to face me, but she wasn't looking at me, she was looking at doing what she had to do. "I'm sorry," she said. "Really, whoever you are. I'm really sorry and I'm really embarrassed too."

"Good," I said. Then she did focus on my face, a brief irritated glance. "Let me get you a cup of coffee, to complete the treatment, and then I'll leave you alone."

That took a minute to sink in. "You're being very kind."

"Very kind," I agreed.

"And patient."

"And patient."

We left the park, crossed over to Madison, and entered the first coffee shop we came to. She wanted to sit at the counter, where she wouldn't have to face me. She wanted to pay. I didn't quarrel with her. She blew over the top of her coffee cup, and sipped. "It's just I'm really embarrassed."

"It's all right," I told her. I had no idea what she was thinking; all I could see was a mass of wormy curls and the mink shoulder. "Believe me, it is."

"I hope I never see you again," she mumbled.

"Yes, well, I can imagine."

"And I feel rotten about hoping that."

"It's only natural."

"I don't even want to know your name. I've probably ruined your whole afternoon too, and all."

She sounded about eighteen years old, and those years cloistered. She sounded young, again, and I couldn't puzzle her out.

"It's all right. You've bought me a cup of coffee, we're almost even."

She let her smile move from her eyes to her mouth. "How about a bagel, would you like a bagel?"

"No, thanks. I had a good lunch."

When she swung around she didn't look eighteen. It was a woman's face, and a woman's wary expression. "That's right, you were in the restaurant. Across. I do remember. I wasn't blotto, just snorkled. Look, I want you to know I don't do this…that. I don't go around drinking too much. I never did before. Although there's no reason for you to believe me, since—but I don't."

Her earnestness required reassurance. "I believe you. I can tell, anyway."

"How?"

"A man knows these things."

She stopped short of outright laughter, but not far. "A man of the world…like yourself."

I nodded agreeably. "A man of the world like myself."

She swung away and lifted her coffee cup. I did the same. The manicure was all wrong for her small hands, nails too bright, too pointed. She was incongruous. The mink was perfect, first-class pelts and tailored for her shortness. Within the mink, she looked dainty and desirable, but the dress...The dress was not a successful effort. She had looked dumpy in the dress, and that hair...but she had wonderful skin, what I could see of it, skin like the traditional peaches and cream, the cream gently warmed. She was beginning to interest me.

"Do you want to talk about it?" I asked. "A stranger is safer to confide in than a friend, it seems to me, sometimes. Cheaper than an analyst—"

Her glance, quick up, then quick down as if to conceal its nature, had the ferocious intelligence of a child. It stopped my words in my throat, it was that quick and clear, gone so suddenly I couldn't be sure I had seen it.

"No, I don't," she said. And smiled at me. "It's too stupid, even I know that. Of course, even though I know that, I don't believe it. Maybe I do want to talk about it. After all, I went out this morning to be remade; this is the new me. So obviously I'm not satisfied with myself as I am. Obviously I want to change my life, so maybe I do want to talk. You're probably right about strangers too. I just don't meet many strangers. What do you think about marriage?" she asked.

"Are you proposing?"

She ignored that as a frivolous response. "Everybody says it's no big deal, you can always get divorced, but I think it's a big deal. And what if you got married because it was the smart thing to do right now, and it turned out dumb? If you meet someone later and really love him, but because you'd done the smart thing...see what I mean?"

"You're romantic."

She shook her head, impatient with me, or with herself, I couldn't tell. "There's an analogy: America and the rest of the world, especially developing nations. The smart thing to do is usually just a euphemism for the expedient—measured in terms of profit, of course—but it's most often shortsighted. Smart, but pretty stupid. I can't figure it out, because it could be something as simple as not being ready. How can I be twenty-nine and not be ready?"

Following her mind was proving a challenge. I opted for moderation. "Give yourself time."

"How old are you?" It was an accusation.

"Thirty-three."

"Really?"

I nodded.

"If I were a man, being that age would make me nervous."

It took me a minute, and then I laughed out loud. "Now that you point it out to me, it does."

"Are you married?"

I shook my head.

"Why not?"

"Not because I haven't been looking."

She nodded her head, as if the conversation was making sense to her. I thought that when I replayed it in my memory I might be able to figure out more about it. For the moment, it was proving difficult enough just to hold up my end, to follow the cues she was giving me.

"I wonder," she said, "why a man wants to marry a woman, a particular woman I mean. It can't be the same as just love. Is it? Men don't marry all the women they fall in love with."

"Marrying someone may be less threatening than loving her."

"What do you mean?" It was that glance again.

"I have an image in my head of stepping into love, and it's like stepping into battle, you know? Gun at the ready, and feeling vulnerable, helpless, wary, under attack—like I said, battle. I'd be a lot less frightened of getting married."

"You've been in love?"

"Once, probably, but I was so young I can't tell how valid it was."

"You're the romantic."

"That's not a bad thing."

"When I first saw you, I took you for older than you are." Now she was facing me, considering me. I wasn't entirely comfortable.

"Well, I try."

"Why?" she asked.

"I took *you* for younger," I said.

"Well, I'm a cliché," she said, mocking my tone of voice. "I wasn't even that drunk, was I? I went out to get drunk and even that I did within safe limits."

"Not a cliché. A romantic. Not to worry."

"I'm not worried." She thought for a moment. "A little embarrassed, and not even too much of that by now, but not worried. I'm ready to go home." She slid off the stool. "Thank you—" and she held out her hand.

I accompanied her. Out on the street, she held her hand out again and got ready to thank me, but I took her elbow and walked her across the street into a flower shop. She didn't know how to stop me, mindful as she was of my courtesy to her and her obligation to feel grateful, so I pinned the little spray of white violets onto her coat and went back outside with her, as if we were together by choice, or at least intention; as if we were together.

People moved around her, distracting her, as she tried again to say her thank-you-and-good-bye. I hailed a cab. "It's for you," I forestalled her protest. "Just you. Alone." I held the door open for her.

She got in and sat back. I still held the door open. It was a contest of wills.

"Where to?" the driver asked me, up through his open window.

I waited. It took her a minute to give in. "Eleven nine-ty-five Park."

She looked me right in the eye as she said it, nothing coy, no attempt to kid herself, and gave me her address. A straight shot.

I handed the driver a bill and repeated the address to him. She had a hand on the door, to pull it closed, and a little speech to deliver before she left. "I'm sorry I thought at first...I probably should have known better. You're a prince, whoever you are, a prince in prince's clothing. Thank you for rescuing me."

3

WHAT THE MACHINE SAID

By the time I had changed my clothes and come back down to the kitchen, the coffee had brewed. I had a cup while I checked the phone messages. Voices on an answering machine are like snapshots, each one separate and singular within its frame of whirrs and beeps.

Whirr, beep. "It's me, Mr. Bear. And if it isn't the most wonderful bear in the world, I don't know who is. These earrings—honestly, I thought they were fake, but I said to myself, 'Mr. Bear wouldn't give anybody fakes, not when they look like this. That's not the kind of guy he is.' They can't be real, but they are, aren't they? I'll let you know tonight how grateful I am. You'll recognize me, I'll be the one in earrings. And nothing else. See you tonight. I'm having some terrific ideas, Mr. Bear." *Beep, whirr.*

Beep. "Ted, the roses are brilliant. Happy Valentine's

Day to you too, lover. I have to be on the West Coast for the next few days but I'll call when I get back. We'll get together. If you want to get ahold of me before then, the office knows where to reach me." *Beep.*

Whirr, beep. "Mr. Mackey's office calling, Mr. Mondleigh. Mr. Mackey wants me to remind you that under the terms of the Trust he can't authorize any such sale. Mr. Mackey suggested that you were, and I quote, 'Trying him on.' If not, he recommends that you make an appointment with him, during which he will advise you about other ways of raising capital, which he suggests—and I quote again—'you know as well as he does.'" *Beep. Whirr.*

Beep. "Ted. Kyle. The court's reserved for nine Saturday. Meet you there." A brief hesitation for thought. "That's nine a.m., Ted."

Beep, whirr, beep. "Nobody, but nobody, has his secretary call to break a date with me. *Nobody.* Good-bye, Mr. Bear, you were real fun for a while." *Beep.*

Whirr, beep. "Teddy? It's Carol Hingham, you probably don't remember me it's been such a long time, Kyle Singleton introduced us…? But if you don't remember, it doesn't matter and besides, I can't jog a memory you don't have, can I? So I—The reason I'm calling is, I'm having a dinner on the twenty-eighth. Nothing much, just a few friends, nothing fancy, just—And I'd love it if you could come. Let me know, OK? 614-3025. I'm a pretty good cook, and I think you'd like my friends, they're pretty interesting people, at least some of them—My number's 614-3025. Did I already say that? I feel like a jerk." She cut herself off. *Beep, whirr,* the machine didn't care how she felt.

Beep. "Lisette here, Teddy. I've never seen a bigger box

of candy. They had to turn it sideways to get it through the door, and I laughed and laughed. Love to you too, Teddy. Give me a call. Soon, hm?"

Beep, whirr, beep, then a hesitating silence. "Hello, Gregor?" I almost jumped. I stared at the black box as if it could actually see me, catch me out. "This is Mrs. Mondleigh speaking. Theo has invited…us to dinner tonight. I'm concerned that he might have forgotten…you. I'm calling to…We can always eat out." *Beep, whirr.*

Beep. "I'm sorry, Mr. Bear, I shouldn't have said that, I know I shouldn't and I'm sorry I did. So I'm calling to say, I just—I got carried away. I guess you know how carried away I can get. Call me quick and say you aren't angry." *Beep.*

Whirr, beep. "There'll be three for dinner, Gregor, it's my parents." *Beep, beep, beep.*

I got to work.

4

INTRODUCING MY EMPLOYER

Theodore Mondleigh was one of the new school of employers, men who look for a certain camaraderie—as long as nobody forgets who is writing the checks. Who has the power to write the checks. When Theodore Mondleigh hired me, he did so with a frank handshake and the expectation that we would "do pretty damned well together."

In fact, what he wanted was someone prematurely stuffy. "I like your dignity, Gregor," he'd said. Unoppressively avuncular. "You'll give the place substance." And a certain éclat. "You've had a pretty broad experience." He could regard me with just enough disdain for both of us to be comfortable. "I don't know why you'd want to spend your life like this, but I assume you know what you're doing, and why. Shall we give it a month's trial?" I had been working for him for almost three years. We were both well satisfied.

Mr. Theo arrived home that Thursday evening at his usual hour. I took his coat at the door. He went straight on back to the kitchen, where I joined him. A nice-looking man, dark blond hair and blue eyes, a short nose and a blunt chin. He moved with the energy of a good athlete, which he was. "Sorry about the short notice, Gregor," he said. "Dad has some bee in his bonnet and wouldn't be put off."

"There was no difficulty," I assured him.

"Not for you maybe. Nothing to be done about it, though. Are there any messages?"

"I left them on the tape."

"I'm going to get a drink first, and listen in here. I'll keep out of your way. How about you, can I get you something?"

I checked the time. "A glass of wine?"

"Red or white?"

"We're having chicken breasts, so white I think. Thank you."

"Thank me?" Mr. Theo laughed. "If it wasn't for you, I'd have to get married."

Mr. Theo sat at the breakfast table listening to the phone messages, sipping at his scotch. I peeled broccoli stems and sliced mushrooms and thought about the day's event.

"My mother doesn't trust me," he remarked.

"Your mother is considerate."

"Oh, well, sure, she's nice, for what that's worth, I just wouldn't like to have to live on what it's worth. If you get me."

I got him.

"You call the Carol person and tell her I can't make

it. She's wrong, I do remember her; if I didn't I might have gone just out of curiosity. She used to hang around with...I can still see the three of them, Bunny and Stick and...Hinge, that's what we called her—Hinge. Hinge, Bunny, and the Stick. Between them they covered about the entire range of female unattractiveness. We weren't exactly friendly with them. I don't know why she's calling me up. Her father was transferred to the Midwest when I was sixteen. I suppose she might have grown up into a raving beauty. Do you think?"

"I have no idea."

"The other two haven't, so probably not. But don't you wonder, Gregor, what it is that attracts all these women? What is it women see in men, what there is about me?"

"Money, sir," I suggested. "Money is a powerful aphrodisiac."

"You're a cynic, Gregor." He stood up. He was almost my height, almost six feet, but he looked shorter because of his tennis player's body. "Kyle told me once that a cynic is just a reformed idealist."

"I would say, rather, a reformed romantic." I was arranging leaves of romaine lettuce on the salad plates.

"That's just words. Anyway, money's not what turns *me* on."

"Yes, well," I said, "perhaps that's because you have so very much of it."

He laughed. "Lucky me then."

"Lucky you."

"I'm going to return that call," he announced, leaving the kitchen. He didn't need to specify which.

• • •

The senior Mondleighs always arrived at precisely ten minutes after the stated time, so I was at the door ready to take their coats when Mr. Theo greeted them. Mr. Mondleigh was a broader version of Mr. Theo, a fine figure of a man. I sometimes think that while it takes only two generations to establish a fortune, the first to make it and the second to test whether it will be—as so many have been—frittered away, it takes at least another two generations to establish the gene pool, the characteristic appearance of the family. Mrs. Mondleigh was another fine figure and as sumptuously presented as her husband, although she didn't command the eye as he did. It was easy to overlook Mrs. Mondleigh, and she seemed to prefer that. Her glance had a luminous quality, a seeing quality, which she concealed by seldom looking directly at people. A hesitant manner of speaking and the softness of her voice concealed her mind. Italian knits with shawl-like tops concealed her body. She was a concealed woman. We got on well.

When I passed around the tray of cheese puffs, the family was in the library. Mrs. Mondleigh stood in front of a Woody, *Interior Landscape #7.* "Did I tell you, Theo, your father and I found one of hers? Not as fine as this, I'm afraid. I don't know how you..." Her voice faded as she searched for the end of her thought.

"Could afford it," Mr. Theo finished for her.

"Recognized its value," Mr. Mondleigh suggested.

She turned to take a cheese puff and say to me, "Of all my children I'd never have thought Theo would be the one to..."

"Have any taste?" Mr. Theo asked. "Actually, Gregor picked it out."

Mr. Mondleigh waved the tray away. "If you ever decide to sell it, I hope you'll give me first refusal."

Mrs. Mondleigh turned her back to them, turned back to the picture.

"I don't think so, Dad."

"You know how your mother likes it."

"If you pressed me, I might consider an offer of twenty thousand."

"That's outrageous," Mr. Mondleigh sputtered. "Gregor? I think I'll change my mind and have one of those things." I returned with the tray. "Have you no family feeling?"

"How about a refill, Dad? I'm ready for one too. Gregor?" I took up the glasses, carrying them to the wet bar. "You have to remember, Dad, that I don't have a profession to fall back on. Living by my wits as I do, I have to keep my eye on any chance to increase my net worth."

"Don't tease your father, Theo," Mrs. Mondleigh murmured.

"I don't know if I'd call cashing a quarterly check from the Trust living by your wits. Consulting, is that what you call what you're doing?"

"Investment counseling, actually," Mr. Theo said.

"For old school friends—thank you, Gregor—who never did a day's work and don't care how much of their fathers', or grandfathers', money you lose."

"You two should never…"

"Well," Mr. Mondleigh said, "Your mother doesn't like arguments."

"They upset her," Mr. Theo agreed.

I went back to the kitchen.

By the soup course, in the fixed procession of conversation at family gatherings, they were discussing relatives and had arrived at Mr. Theo's younger sister, the baby of the family, "due home at the end of April, and I hope the year abroad has taught her some sense. Or at least that the school has taught her to be more manageable."

I set the double-handled bowls of bouillon down gently.

"Does that mean you'll cut short your stay in the Bahamas?" Mr. Theo asked. "Or will she join you there?"

"Sarah hasn't let us know…"

"Her plans," Mr. Theo said, amused. "Sarah doesn't like plans. She's a free spirit, she knows how to stop and smell the roses. It's too late to try and change her."

"I'll feel a lot easier in my mind when she's married and has a couple of children to settle her down," Mr. Mondleigh agreed.

The main course of the meal was the time for the main focus of the gathering: Mr. Theo himself.

"…a man of your age," Mr. Mondleigh was saying as I entered. I offered the platter of sautéed chicken breasts to Mrs. Mondleigh, then Mr. Mondleigh, then Mr. Theo.

After that, I carried around rice pilaf encircled by minted baby carrots.

"I'm only thirty, Dad. That's not what anyone would call old."

"You can't blame the boy, David, if he doesn't want to…"

"Grow up? I certainly can. And I do."

I adjusted the platter so that Mrs. Mondleigh could take the serving spoon.

"Can't we drop the subject?" Mr. Theo asked.

"Not until you give me some good reason. At thirty, your brother had two sons and was expecting his third child. I'm not even going to mention where his career was at that age, except to say he was the youngest Assistant Head in Groton's history."

"You're lucky to have one entirely satisfying son, Dad. One is more than a lot of men get. You should be grateful."

"The Rawlings are a fine family, we've known them all your life, you know everything about her," Mr. Mondleigh said. He made his points like a carpenter, first setting then settling a nail. He seemed to think that the more convinced he was, the more convincing his arguments would be. As if conviction made them true.

"Dad," Mr. Theo protested, at the same time that his mother spoke softly, "David."

The kitchen door swung closed behind me.

For dessert, I brought an apple tart to the table, and three plates with cut wedges served on them. Mr. Theo had by then become mocking. "You're saying I should get married because you're ready for me to be married?"

"She's a thoroughly nice girl," his father answered. "Quiet, bookish. What do you have against her?"

Mrs. Mondleigh reached out a hand to her son. She didn't touch him, but she reached out, an uncompleted gesture. "Are you in love with someone, Theo?"

"Are you saying I should get married because I'm not in love with anyone?"

I had dishes to wash.

The dishwasher was loaded, the pots and pans scoured and dried and put away, the dirty silverware piled beside a sink by the time Mrs. Mondleigh brought the tart platter into the kitchen. I dried my hands.

"Dinner was delicious, as always, Gregor," she said.

"Thank you, Mrs. Mondleigh. I'll serve coffee in the living room."

"If I were a…"

I poured coffee into the silver pot, and waited.

"…less loving mother, I'd try to hire you away."

"I'm very well suited here," I told her.

She smiled. "I should think so. I would think working for Theo is…"

I picked up the tray, and waited.

"…a plum."

"A plum indeed."

• • •

As I entered the living room, I saw that Mr. Theo's nostrils were flaring in anger, a restrained quivering, like the rims of oysters simmering in a stew. He sat in an armchair, facing his father, who sat in an identical chair facing him. Mrs. Mondleigh had placed herself on the sofa, between them. "Most of the young men your age are married," Mr. Mondleigh said. He was not angry, because he was sure he was right.

"Most for the second time," Mr. Theo countered.

I put the tray down on a side table and poured three cups.

"Is that supposed to be funny? Because I don't find it particularly humorous. You're too young to know it, but love is about the worst possible basis for marriage. I wasn't—thank you, Gregor"—he took the cup and set it down without a glance at it—"in love with your mother when we married. If I were being candid, I'd have to say I didn't even start to love her until Davy was born. And we've been married almost thirty-six years now; we have a marriage that's lasted. By now, by this time…well. Love isn't something you fall into, son. It's something you grow into."

Mr. Theo drank from his cup, glaring at his father over the rim. I offered Mrs. Mondleigh sugar and cream.

"That first year, your mother could have been anyone, any reasonably attractive, eligible girl. It didn't require love. You're old enough, and experienced enough, to—"

Mr. Theo's nostrils flared.

I had their coats ready as the senior Mondleighs went to the door. Mr. Mondleigh went out first to bring the car from the garage. I held Mrs. Mondleigh's heavy mink for her. She had her eyes on her husband's broad back, descending the steps to the sidewalk, walking away. "Do you know, Theo, I was so in love with him I thought I'd die if he didn't ask me to marry him. I thought I would actually die. It's funny to think that…"

Mr. Theo finished the sentence for her. "Things might have been so different, with a different choice. I know what you mean, Mother."

"But that wasn't…" She reached up to kiss his cheek. "Well, perhaps I was more naive than most. I was surely more…naive than girls are now. Thank you again, Gregor."

I bowed my head and withdrew.

I was sitting at the kitchen table drying the silver when Mr. Theo entered. "It looks like I have to be out at the Farm this Saturday." He sat down in the other chair, then sprawled back. "They're putting the pressure on. Heavy pressure."

"I did notice."

"Well? What do you think? You're not married. How old are you, Gregor? Why aren't you married?"

"Thirty-three."

"I knew that, didn't I? It was on your CV. I just always think of you as older, I don't know why. It's not that you actually look older."

"It's part of my job, sir. To appear older."

"Whatever Dad says, I'd rather make money on my own. He might be contented as long as he doesn't lose what he's inherited, but that's not good enough for me. They've even picked out the girl."

"What does *she* think of it?" I added a gleaming serving spoon to the line of silverware in front of me.

"Prune?" he asked.

I was alarmed. As a non sequitur it had its perfection, but I was accustomed to being able to follow his thought processes. "Prune?" I asked.

Mr. Theo laughed, bright boyish laughter. "That's what we called her, Davy and me, whenever—We had to play with her sometimes, and she'd just, just stand around, lips pursed, like this. She disapproved of everything about us. The way we talked and the games we liked and—We did pick on her, I guess, poor Pruny, all dressed up. She was always dressed up, Mary Janes and sashes; she always did what she was told. She was a good girl. She's not my type at all. I mean, *really* not my type, Gregor, I don't know what my parents are thinking, what dream world they're living in, or what century."

I rubbed the pie server and said nothing. He sighed deeply, a sigh of manly resignation.

"You know what I mean," he said.

I thought I probably did.

"There's a dance at the Club on Saturday, a Valentine dance. Black tie, a dinner dance, they've exhumed Lester Lanin I think, for the occasion. Prune's going, with her parents of course. I don't remember ever seeing her without her parents in attendance. I guess you wouldn't get an unpleasant disease from that kind of girl, and I suppose, these days, that's something, but—Have you ever been married, Gregor?"

"No."

"It's appalling what my parents think they can do, isn't it?"

"A distinctly Eastern way of thinking, sir."

"And why don't you just run the silver through the dishwasher?"

"It takes years of polishing to give silver this luster," I told him. "Like wearing pearls is what gives them their tone."

"I won't do it, anyway."

"Get married?"

"They can't force me to it, that's something. It's not as if I need her money. You know"—he sat up, sat forward, struck by insight—"they're all stereotypes, Connecticut stereotypes. You've never seen them, Gregor, but the Rawlings are serious gardeners. I mean, serious, serious gardeners. And Pruny is their prize begonia. Or prize potato, that's more like her. It's her being their prize performance, I mean, and they hover behind, looking modestly good, rewarded by wealth and position…You know what I mean? All very Episcopalian, of course, nothing in bad taste. I'm not kidding, Gregor."

"I didn't think you were, sir."

"My family too," he said. "There's Dad, trying to keep anything from changing, ever—as if he actually could. He goes to his board meetings, he reads the reports—You know, the guy never practiced law? He went right from law school to boards of directors. Without passing Go, without picking up his two hundred dollars, which he didn't need, and that makes the difference. But he has no idea. And my mother, she—A woman who can't finish half her own sentences. She makes other people do everything—finish her sentences, manage her money, decorate her houses, pick the restaurants. And Sarah, coming home from that Italian school: she'll show horses and play golf and after a while she'll get married. It's enough to choke a man to death. The whole life. The whole family. Davy perpetuating the good genes, perpetuating the institutions. But—" He was too discouraged to go on. "What can you do? It's still pretty early. I think I'll make a phone call. I may be going out." He got up from the chair.

"Will you be wanting the car, sir?" I asked.

"You're kidding," Mr. Theo said.

"I'm kidding."

He stared down at me for a minute. "You're as much a stereotype as the rest of us, Gregor."

"I know, sir," I told him, pleased. "Have a good evening."

I thought I knew where he'd be going and why he didn't want to drive. There was no danger that he'd be back soon. When I finished in the kitchen, I hung my apron up and went upstairs to change. You can never be too careful.

It was early enough in the evening to make it easy to find a cab. I directed the driver to 1195 Park, and sat back to see what I might be getting myself into.

The cab pulled over in front of a four-story building with a Georgian proportion to the windows and the single entrance. I could see beside the door none of the plaques that announce the presence of doctors, dentists, or psychiatrists. The smooth facade of the building rose from the sidewalk like a stone wall. A few of the long windows on the second floor glowed faintly, light behind heavy curtains. It seemed to me likely that this was a private residence. There were several ways for me to find out if it was, and I thought I would try the most amusing one. When I'd looked my fill, I rolled the window up and directed the cabbie to take me home.

5

FROGGY GOES COURTING

Not that I had a plan worked out, a schedule of fixed progression from cause to consequence, hope to happy ending. All I had was an idea of how I might go about it, more instinct than skill. Previous experience would guide me only so far, since each experience has only its own distinctive qualities. All I knew was what my next step would be.

I selected what struck me as the best bet from the *Times* that Sunday, and on Monday afternoon I stood in front of 1195 Park. I held in my hand a small white box, which contained a bouquet of white violets and, in the envelope, half of a pair of tickets to the Sunday afternoon performance of some Mozart horn concertos. My idea is that men prefer Bach and Handel, while women will choose Beethoven, Wagner, the Russians. Guessing at what will please regardless of gender, I always choose Mozart.

I ascended the staircase, rang, and waited, the little white box in my hand. I heard no sound from within, not even the muffled call of the bell. After a time, the door opened. A butler, entirely correct from his polished shoes to his smooth white hair, looked me over. "Sir?" he inquired.

"I'd like to leave these for the young lady." I gave him the box and stepped back, to assure him that I wasn't asking admittance.

His face gave away nothing of whatever he might have been thinking. "Very good, sir," he told me. The thick wood of the door thunked closed.

There was always the chance that she wouldn't risk it. My thought was that she would use the week to make up her mind; my hope was that she would make up her mind in my favor. Her first reaction would be that it was impossible, but she could, if she wanted to, talk herself out of that misapprehension—given time. If she didn't want to... That was the key, what she wanted. She hadn't struck me as impulsive, so time would work in my favor, I judged. Her quality was not naiveté but unsophistication, probably lack of experience rather than ignorance. I gave her the week to think me over. I was banking on her innocence.

She arrived at the last minute. My smile of greeting was dying a natural death before she had stumbled apologetically over the legs between us to sit down and finally meet my eyes. She'd altered her hair: straightened, it was brushed back from her face except for the long bangs, which wisped down as if left there by a wind. It still looked like somebody else's hair, or maybe a wig, the right haircut for somebody else's face, a face with a ready smile, confidently flirtatious eyes, an upturned nose, and a plump, kissable mouth. Not her face. Her face was narrow, oval, her nose had more boniness to it, and her mouth, while not ungenerous, was solemn. She must have left her coat at the cloakroom; she carried only a purse, blue like her schoolgirl jumper. Her nails were unpainted and the only makeup she wore was a pale lipstick. Her skin glowed like pearls.

"I'm sorry I'm late," she murmured. After that first glance she wouldn't look at me.

"You're not late, you're right on time." The musicians proved my words, entering as if on cue. They bowed, seated themselves, arranged music on stands. She bent to put her purse on the floor.

When the concerto started, she fell still. I watched her surreptitiously for the opening bars, but I needn't have bothered with stealth. She seemed to have forgotten me entirely, and forgotten her discomfiture too. She sat quietly, legs crossed at the ankles, skirt spread over her knees, hands resting in one another's gentle clasp in her lap. But her face responded to the music, to Mozart, eyes and mouth, unselfconscious as a child. Until the melody and harmony took me, I watched her listen.

There was no intermission, just a brief period of applause between concertos, the audience impatient to return to its interrupted pleasure. Whether the horn was leading the other instruments on a chase like Puck mocking the Athenian lovers, or singing its siren's song to lure them onto immolating rocks, the music played around us, played with us, and I felt as if I were myself one of the horn's attendant instruments. I forgot everything, and listened.

The real applause came at the end, and she was smiling without any thought of where she was or who she was with. "Let's wait until the crowd clears a little," I suggested, and she nodded her agreement, clapping. When the stage was emptied and conversation rose around us, I remarked, "That was worth listening to."

"Yes," she said, still watching the now-empty stage. Then she made herself face me. "That was nice of you. Do you often do that? Deliver concert tickets to damsels in distress?"

"Are you still in distress?"

It was the wrong question, the wrong topic. Quickly, I tried another. "I didn't know if you'd come. I didn't know if you have a sister."

"No sister. What if I hadn't? What would you have thought?"

"That you didn't like concerts. Or you didn't like Mozart. Or you didn't like me. Or that you had a previous engagement." At least I had amused her. "You changed your hair."

She nodded. "I remembered you darker," she said.

"That was the suit." For Sunday afternoon I wore light gray.

"If you wanted to seem safe, a safe person? A concert would be a good cover," she said.

"I'm glad to see you have some sense," was the response I chose to that.

"It's not very nice of you to remind me."

"No, it's not."

"I'm not as bad as you think." Before I could tell her I didn't think she was bad at all, she informed me, "I'm being met. Out front." Then she heard the connotation. "I don't mean to insult you."

"I'm not insulted." A little disappointed, yes, but it was no more than I expected.

"I don't know what you planned—"

"I didn't plan anything. A concert, with you. You listen so intently—It's revealing, how a person listens to music."

The thought alarmed her at first and then interested her. She had a face that gave away what she was thinking, that she *was* thinking. "There's a kind of intimacy, isn't there?"

"Much more dangerous than the usual kind," I pronounced. "I think that might be true," I added. "I think I might believe that."

"Like, if two people are reading together, it's personal?"

"Intensely personal. Reading together in bed, now that must be the most intimate thing I can think of."

She laughed, relaxed now. Most of the audience had left but we weren't the only ones sitting, talking. "*Do* you do this often?" she asked again.

"I think maybe not often enough." It had gone well, I thought. It had been the right move. We were turned to face one another in our seats.

"All right," she said, "don't tell me anything," bringing me up short. It wouldn't do to underestimate her. "I can't think what to talk about. I don't even know what business you're in."

"If business is all we can find to talk about, then we won't be friends." I selected the word carefully.

"Or family? Your family? You must have a family." She waited, unable to read my face. "You know, a mother and a father."

"I have a mother and a father."

"You don't want to talk about them?"

I shook my head but picked up her cue. "You also must have a family, parents."

She shook her head, and her mouth was serious although her eyes had mischief in them. "Well," she said, retrieving her purse, "thank you for a lovely concert."

I half rose in my seat, just as I had done to greet her, to let her know that I wouldn't importune her but that she could count on my desire to see her again as well as my good manners. "It was my pleasure. Thank you for coming, for risking it."

That pleased her, which was my intention. She moved down the row and then up the aisle, trying not to show that she was aware I was watching, the little purse bobbing at her side. I waited for several minutes before I followed.

The next afternoon I got myself togged out and went down to Ludovic's Ticket Agency, where Mrs. Wallace was, as always, stoutly ensconced behind the desk in the cubbyhole office. There was no Ludovic, Mrs. Wallace being the sole proprietor and sole employee. When I'd explained what I wanted, Mrs. Wallace made a phone call. Mrs. Wallace seldom had to make more than one phone call to get what she was looking for.

If I wanted an entire box for a Sunday matinee, I would have to wait three weeks. A long time, I thought, then, perhaps just the right length of time. "You could have *All for Love* next week," Mrs. Wallace told me, while the box office waited at the other end of the line.

"No, it's *Twelfth Night* I want." I took out my checkbook while she completed arrangements.

She wrote out the bill, at ninety dollars a seat plus her ten percent commission. I wrote out the check. "The tickets will be here by tomorrow afternoon, Mr. Rostov," she said. "The reviews have been quite favorable." Mrs. Wallace, I had learned, rode home to Queens by subway and preferred TV to live theater. She had never seen a Broadway show, or an Off-Broadway, she confided once; but she studied the reviews, so she could advise a client who didn't know his own mind. Or hers.

When I returned the next day to pick up the envelope, I waited until I was back on the street to take out four of the tickets and rip them into little pieces. I didn't want to offend Mrs. Wallace's sensibilities, or sense of propriety, or self-image. One of the two remaining tickets I returned to the little envelope. I waited two days before I delivered it to 1195 Park, for the young lady, accompanied by a nosegay of white violets.

I had, I thought, some reason to hope.

6

THE WINDS OF MARCH

On the first Monday in March, Mr. Theo arrived home an hour early. "A foul day."

I looked on the bright side. "It's not sleet."

"What is it, the third day of this? I get stir-crazy, like a rat in a cage." Rain gusted against the kitchen windows, beating gray against glass before sliding dismally down it. "I've invited some people in for drinks, no more than a dozen, but what about dinner?"

"Dinner won't stretch to twelve, sir."

He wasn't surprised. "We can eat out."

I put the lamb chops away and brought out cheeses. I had spicy meatballs in the freezer—they could be microwaved—and vegetables to cut up with dip; there were nuts.

"Maybe I'll take a week off, go to the islands. Would you like a week in the islands, Gregor?"

"You wouldn't want my company."

"No, I wouldn't." He laughed. "Not that I find you an inhibiting presence."

"I would hope not."

The rain hammered at the glass.

"Although," he turned around to look at me, "you don't encourage me either. Neutral, that's what you are. I couldn't do that, I couldn't be so neutral."

"A euphemism," I suggested.

"Not in the bad sense," Mr. Theo said. "I'll get the bar set up in the living room. Is there a fire laid? When I've changed, and don't worry about the door, I'll get it. You just go ahead with whatever."

Mr. Theo served the first round of drinks, then stood beside the fire. I passed platters of food, offered refills for drinks, and waited beside the bar, ready and invisible. Five women and six men were scattered standing and sitting around the room. The men wore woolen slacks, Aran or Scandinavian or Icelandic sweaters, and duck shoes. They laid claim to individuality in their drinks: one dark German beer, one light Dutch, one Canadian, one vodka martini, and one sipping whiskey. Mr. Theo drank scotch.

The women all held glasses of wine but varied in their dress. One was a female counterpart of the men, in brown slacks and an Aran sweater of the cardigan type; another wore a long skirt and gypsy blouse; there was a jeweled lady whose ears and fingers, arms and chest were spotted with a mix of fine and junk-store gems; one woman wore a severely tailored suit. And one woman—One woman was beautiful, a scrotum-tightening beauty, out of place in that room, gleaming like the barrel of a gun. A model, I thought, almost sure I'd seen her on a magazine cover. Her facial bones were so delicate that I thought if you kissed her soundly, with a hand at the back of her head, you might crush her skull. You might want to.

Not unaware that they were in the presence of beauty, the men discussed the question of the real national sport, a contest between baseball (the historical argument), football (the argument by profitability), and basketball (the under-dog). The women took no part but leaned forward with interest, except for the model, whose blue-green eyes made no pretense of enjoyment or thought.

Then they got down to the serious business of the evening's entertainment, and conversation became more general. I carried around offerings of meatballs, vegetables, cheese; I poured glasses of wine, beer, liquor. They consid-ered their options, questing for the inspiration that would lead them to delight. As always with a group, they moved toward consensus, the trail marked by predictable turns.

Dinner: "We're not dressed for Le Cirque; they'd never let us in."

"Yes, they would, but anyway, I hate being *allowed* into places."

A show: "We'll never be able to get eleven tickets, not at this hour."

An exotic dinner: "I know an Indian restaurant, down on First Avenue, there's almost an Indian district there, that might be fun."

Activities of the sporting kind: "Nobody wants to play round-robin tennis tonight, Kyle."

"Or watch football, and especially not in a bar," one of the women announced. "Besides, I have to go to work tomorrow morning."

"Well, so do I."

"Yeah, but the place where I work isn't named after my grandfather."

An eccentricity: "Anybody else here like jazz?"

A film: "Not another foreign movie."

And a consensus: "It should be sleazy. No, I'm serious, listen. This is the perfect weather for sleazy, right? We could go down to Forty-Second Street and have kielbasas on rolls and catch an X-rater. I bet that's something some of us haven't done."

"That's not exactly a safe part of town, Teddy."

"But there are so many of us, and besides, you told me you've never seen one, and you wished you could. This way, you'd get the full ambience of the occasion, much realer than renting one and watching it at home. Kyle and I did it lots, didn't we, Kyle? When we were at New Haven."

"I don't know if I want to. But if I chicken out, I'll probably hate myself in the morning."

The men leaned toward one another, conferring. "We'll need cash. Leave the credit cards here; how much cash do we have?"

The women leaned toward one another, conferring, "Are you OK with this?" "I guess if all of us…"

The men emptied their wallets and pockets onto the coffee table. The fire crackled.

"In that case I'll say good night," the model announced.

She stood and brushed her long hair back over her shoulder. "Thanks for the drink, Teddy."

"Wait, Mako." Mr. Theo put a hand on her naked arm. "You don't want to see a porno flick?"

She smiled. "Got it in one, sonny. I like my men turned on over me, not…That is, if I want to turn them on. I like to get the credit." She looked around the room. "And the fun."

It was a showstopper. The men froze in place. You could almost see them licking their lips. My own lips could have used moistening. Neither were the women immune to the sudden thickening of the air: each shifted away from the others, isolating herself, eyes gleaming.

It took a few seconds for everyone to return to life.

"Wait, I don't care about a skin flick. What would *you* like to do?" they asked her.

1

TWELFTH NIGHT

From a box seat you get an overhead view of the audience, much as you do of the stage. It is almost as if there are two stages on view from a box seat, one which thinks it is real and the other which knows it is artificial. We lingered, leaning our elbows on the railing, watching first the stage empty and then the theater.

She wore a Liberty dress, a print of tiny flowers in various shades of pink, with a touch of lace at the collar and smocking at the wrists. I wore smoky gray and my tie was quietly opulent. "Maybe," she said, picking up a conversation we had left at the end of the last intermission, "we accept Viola and Sebastian as indistinguishable twins—no matter how different they look—because we want to believe it."

"Willing suspension of disbelief?"

"But doesn't it feel as if Shakespeare wants to force us to understand what we're doing? Force us to do it, then to know we're doing it because we want the story. Otherwise"—her light-brown eyes were troubled—"why does he put them together on stage in that last scene? Face to face like that. When you have to see that they never could have been mistaken for one another. But you have to accept that they have been if you want the story to happen." She looked at me. "I'm sorry."

Sorry for ignoring my attempt to enter the conversation, sorry for talking so much, sorry for choosing her own ideas over mine: I didn't know which, and I suspected those options barely scratched the surface of some general apology, her letter to the world which read in its entirety "I'm sorry." I ignored the apology and addressed her thoughts.

"Maybe he did it because he could. I mean, he could pull it off. It shouldn't work, and it does. It's implausible and we believe it. Can you imagine how it would feel to be able to do that?" I could, and it made me smile.

She shook her head; my answer wasn't good enough. "The play begins with music and love—"

"Ends with a song," I offered.

"But not a love song. And all the couples, at the end, at the happy ending, they're all based on misapprehensions. Or deceptions."

"The fool has the envoi," I said, in case that helped.

She shook her head again. "Well."

She was getting ready to leave, reaching for her purse, preparing her thanks and farewells. I made no move.

She looked around the box, at the four empty chairs. "You don't cut corners, do you?"

"Not for you." I gave it a little time, very little, just a beat, then said, "I don't know your name."

"No, you don't."

"That's all right," I assured her at the same time that she said, "It's not that—" and stopped. I should have kept my mouth shut, I thought. I should have been more patient. I wondered how she might have ended her sentence but couldn't ask now, and it was now too late for waiting to hear what lead she might have given me. I fetched our coats from the anteroom.

"I've enjoyed your company," I told her, holding the mink out for her arms. "Once again."

"And I thank you once again." She fastened up the frogs.

"You're being met?" If I seemed to be trying to pin her down, I'd lose whatever ground I'd gained by not trying to pin her down. "Because I'd like to have dinner with you. Or tea—it's about the right time for high tea. Tea's a respectable occasion, safe."

"I can't," she said.

"Or a cup of coffee, somewhere close by."

"I'm being met. It's just…I don't know anything about you," she apologized.

"So you have to take me on faith."

"Yes," she said, serious. "Or not at all."

"Or not at all."

Then her mood lifted. "But you can't know, this has been—a respite, *Twelfth Night*, seeing it. Seeing it with you, that too. You don't know, but it's just what I needed."

"That's good news," I said, and meant it. I sat down again so she could leave. She didn't hurry, she didn't delay, and before she let the door close behind her she smiled at me, uncertainly.

8

WHAT THE MACHINE SAID

I was unloading grocery bags—cleaning supplies for the crew of four who came every two weeks to take care of floors and windows; a few bottles of wine; green shrimp for a scampi—listening to the phone messages.

Beep. "Mr. Wilkerson at Sulka's calling. The suits Mr. Mondleigh ordered are ready to be picked up." *Beep. Whirr.*

I checked the time; I could fetch them that day, if I hurried.

Beep. "You are adorable, Mr. Bear," the familiar voice, low and rough-edged, like a cat's purr. "Absolutely adorable. Even a non-Irish girl loves emeralds. I know it's a couple of days early, but I could make a pitcher of green beer—if you wanted. I'll be here all afternoon, in case you felt like calling. I've got no plans for tonight. So if you'd like to do something? I'm available." *Beep. Whirr.*

My instructions were not to call Mr. Theo at the office except in case of emergency; this was no emergency message, although the voice, vibrating, implied a certain urgency. I grinned, and laid a bottle into the wine rack.

Beep. "Theodore Mondleigh. You don't know me. My name is Rothman, Howard Rothman. From Minneapolis. I have a software company that does business with Hal Patricks. Hal gave me your number, and from what he says I'm interested in talking to you. I'll be in town Monday; I'm booked into the Hilton all week. It sounds like we both might make some money, so give me a call and we'll set something up. It's Friday, eleven fifteen my time." *Beep. Whirr.*

Again, I checked the time, picturing the sun making its arced way over a map of the United States to figure out whether I should be adding or subtracting an hour, then gave myself a mental shake: what did the time matter? Why was I so concerned with the time?

Beep. "Theo? Your father wants you here in time for lunch tomorrow…something about papers he wants you and Davy to look at. That's the first thing. Do you remember, we're having dinner with the Rawlings? Be sure to pack something appropriate. They're more…formal than we are. Oh, and Davy said he'd like a game of squash Sunday morning. I'll book a court. There was one more thing…but I can't remember. I hope it wasn't important." *Beep.*

Distracted by hopefulness: that explained me to myself. I was counting days until…

Whirr. Beep. "Teddy? If you can't make it Saturday, how about Tuesday for dinner? It's been too long, much too long. You'll love hearing about my new job—it's a giggle, I promise. But you've been hard to get ahold of for the last two or three weekends. What's going on? Anything interesting? Oh, it's Muffy." *Beep. Whirr.*

I remembered Muffy. Muffy was fluffy, that was why I remembered her. Mr. Theo's affiliation might have been Episcopalian, but his tastes were Catholic.

Beep. "Theo? I remembered, your father wants a general outline of your will. He's rewriting his. I hope...you don't mind?" *Beep. Whirr.*

Well, hope springs eternal.

Beep. "Gregor? I won't be in for dinner. Don't wait up." *Beep, beep, beep.*

Which meant that he didn't plan to be home that night. I looked at the mound of raw shrimp—more than I could eat on my own. A De Jonghe certainly wouldn't freeze, but with the shells still on, although not as tender as fresh, still, in a shallot-tomato sauce, over a pasta...It is the lack of waste I admire most in French kitchens. If you live in New York, you have to know how close we are to being buried by our own garbage, and you may even think it serves us right.

I thought I could get the shrimp wrapped and into the freezer before I headed over to Sulka's, and double-checked the time.

9

IMPROVISATIONS ON A THEME

While I waited to know if she would risk a third meeting, Mr. Theo accelerated his social life, which kept me busy and I was not ungrateful. Ten days pass quickly when your skills are being challenged. This period began with a standing rib roast on an evening of gusty, dark March rains.

I opened the door to Mr. Theo and saw that he had a woman with him. Behind them, the limousine drove off. I took his umbrella, their raincoats, and her rain hat. She was an ash blonde, blue-eyed, with a rangy golfer's build. He greeted me formally. "Good evening, Gregor."

"Good evening, sir."

"Will dinner stretch to one more? We don't want to go out again, do you?"

"Not likely," she said. "Not in this weather."

"There's a roast for dinner," I told him. "More than enough."

"Good. Let's have a drink. How does that sound to you, Holly?"

"Absolutely great. It sounds absolutely perfect."

He put a hand on the small of her back to guide her into the library. I hung up their rainwear, made the necessary alterations to the table, and opened a bottle of burgundy to accompany the standing rib roast.

Beef Stroganoff, its sour-creamy gravy shot through with fresh dill, was what I served the next night to Mr. Theo and a redhead. Molly, I named her, after Sweet Molly Malone, because of her easy laugh and her large, strong-looking hands. For breakfast she wanted juice, fresh-squeezed if I could manage that, and eggs, and scrapple if I had any but bacon would do, and toast, and fried potatoes if that was all right.

Cold beef in thin slices—the day was unseasonably warm—is what I set down before Mr. Theo and a curly-haired brunette I called Dolly, for her Kewpie mouth. Folly ate roast beef hash with a flash of rings—wedding ring, engagement ring, and the odd blockbuster sapphire—and gave me an occasional predatory glance as if to say that when she had finished with Mr. Theo...Polly, with her long honey-blonde hair and visible gladness, ate shepherd's pie and talked about how incredibly lucky she was to have gotten the job she held, the apartment she shared with a cousin, an evening with Mr. Theo all to herself.

The beef went quickly. Turkey—tetrazzini, hash, capilotade, curry—lasted no longer. Time flies when you are working hard.

On the Saturday morning before the Sunday afternoon I was waiting for, a recently shaven Mr. Theo sat at the kitchen table, drinking his morning tomato juice, looking altogether fresh and pink and pleased. I had a pan of bacon frying.

"Will the young lady want breakfast?"

"I took the young lady home a few hours ago. Some young ladies, Gregor, feel compromised if they stay the night."

"And how would you like your eggs?"

"Scrambled, I think. Yes, scrambled."

"We have finished with the turkey, sir. Should I procure a leg of lamb?"

"Do I detect a note of disapproval?"

He wasn't really inquiring. I didn't really answer. I whisked eggs. "If anything, a note of admiration."

Mr. Theo laughed, but I didn't turn around. "You're pure gold, Gregor. I have an impulse to give you a raise, but that would be the action of a man who felt guilty. And I don't."

"I don't need a raise."

"But you're right about me. I don't know what's gotten into me. Which isn't to say I'm not having a fine time, because I am, I'm having a fine old time. And it's not as if I'm not taking reasonable precautions..."

"I'm glad to hear that, sir. This is no time to be cavalier about sexually transmitted diseases."

"You can say that again," he said. I didn't. "You know what I think? I think it's the idea of marriage. That, and all the family weekends out at the Farm, it makes me...horny? No, incredibly randy, that's what it is. I can't pass anyone by, I can't say no to anyone. I'm not saying it's not fun, but—Does this make any sense to you?"

"Will you be getting married then?" I transferred the eggs to a plate and laid strips of bacon beside them. I added buttered toast to the plate.

"Good God, no. The parents are putting on the pressure, but I hold firm. All very civilized, of course, nothing actually stated, just family get-togethers—as if the Rawlings were their best friends or long-lost cousins or something. I don't know what poor Pruny makes of it, although she doesn't seem to care what goes on around her. I never know what she thinks. But I tell you what, Gregor. It'll be a relief when the parents go off on vacation next week. Four weeks of peace, and privacy." He munched on a slice of toast. "I don't know what time tomorrow I'll be able to get away. There's always a big lunch on Sunday."

"I'll leave something cold for you, shall I?"

"Gregor?" He looked up from his breakfast. "What do you do on your days off? I suppose you must have a private life?"

I wasn't going to tell him, and he didn't want to know. Instead I asked, "Isn't that the proper order of things? I'm supposed to know everything about you, and you're supposed to know nothing about me."

"I know you're probably better educated than I am," Mr. Theo agreed, "and we both know you've got better taste."

"That also is the proper order of things, isn't it?"

"You *are* a cynic."

"I'm afraid not, sir."

10

A GOLDEN FLUTE

We had left the church together, left the concert together, and stood together on the steps where earlier I had waited for her. She wore a kilt and walking shoes and a down vest, looking like the many other women there who had hurried in from the country to hear Rampal play a benefit for African refugees. I was still dazed by the memory of the bobbing figure, and the notes as golden as his flute moving through the church like sunlight through leaves. She had sat with what I was beginning to recognize as a typical attentive stillness. Now we stood in the last of the late-afternoon sunlight. I could hear remembered music more clearly than the sounds of city life around us. I put my thought into words. "Wonderful."

"Unmn," she answered, then changed the topic. "You listen with your shoulders."

"What?"

"Your shoulders…move. With the music. Maybe your neck too, chin. It's not unseemly. You're never unseemly," she teased me.

I came back to the real world and wondered if this was the moment for the next step.

"I'm always saying thank you," she said, holding out her hand for me to shake.

I didn't take it. "And walking away."

"Yes." She put both hands into the waist-high pockets. "I don't know *what* James thinks."

"James?"

"Our butler. He calls you the Gentleman. 'The Gentleman left this for you, miss.'" It was a fair imitation of his voice, redolent with nasal dignity, and I laughed.

"Does it matter what James thinks?" I asked.

"No."

"What do you think?"

"I don't know what to think. So I don't. I enjoy your company, and the things you ask me to do."

"Am I good enough company to take you to dinner?" It was time to try, to at least try.

"I can't," she said quickly.

"I'll walk you home though. It's all right, I already know where you live. I won't go to the door, just stand on the corner until you're inside. See you safely home."

She considered that, then nodded her head, agreeing to it. "You're old-fashioned, aren't you?"

"I'm afraid maybe I am."

11

WHAT THE MACHINE SAID

I had purchased a spring bouquet, on impulse—little irises, a few tulips, daffodils—and trimmed their stalks under running water. While I was arranging them in a clear glass vase I listened to the few messages on the answering machine. Once the flowers were displayed, I'd think about where to put them.

Beep. "Theo? It's Mother. To remind you about tomorrow, the opera. We'll meet you at the box. You two might... have dinner, before." *Beep, whirr.*

Beep. "Lisette here. Any man I don't hear from for five weeks I'm finished with. The men I respect at least call up, to say it's over. That's the way I like it. That's the only way I take it. Good-bye, Teddy Mondleigh."

Beep, whirr, beep. "Mr. Bear, I haven't seen you for eight days. And I miss you, I honestly do. Are you gonna call me up or anything? Is something wrong, did I do something wrong?" *Beep*.

Whirr, beep. "Hi, Teddy, it's Bonnie, and thank you for the dinner and everything. Any time you'd like to do it again, you know where to find me." *Beep, beep, beep*.

The flowers I put on the kitchen table, where they shone bright against the gray window. The flowers—I hadn't understood it—were for me.

12

A NIGHT AT THE OPERA

I could have envied Mr. Theo his dressing room. Paneled in golden oak, it was an affair of closets—closets to hold hanging clothes, closets fronting for caned drawers, and one closet that opened into a floor-length three-way tailor's mirror. Recessed lighting and the thick brown carpet soft under a bare foot...Enviable.

Ordinarily I was only responsible to care for Mr. Theo's wardrobe, but when he had a black-tie occasion, I played valet. It wasn't that he couldn't put in his own studs, tie his own tie, slip his own feet into the patent-leather shoes; he simply preferred me to hold ready the parts of his ensemble, one after the other, and pass them to him at the proper time. I didn't fault him. We were playing out a scene; the mirrors reflected us, man and manservant. Mr. Theo had said as much to me, one of the first times I valeted him that way. "I feel like royalty."

Looking at our reflections, I had remarked, "Royalty, or a woman. Women must feel that way." The air between us had become immediately tense, charged.

"You're not gay, are you, Gregor?" If I had been, and wanted to keep the job, I'd have denied it; as it was I simply denied it. "Bisexual?"

"No."

He wanted to ask more, the next logical step, but didn't quite dare. What, I had wondered, looking at his reflections, would his reaction be if I asked him the same set of questions.

That evening, as I held out the starched dress shirt, Mr. Theo remarked, "Many gentlemen wear turtlenecks with their tuxes." He worked the studs up the front of his shirt.

"I'm sure many gentlemen do." I dropped the next stud into his hand.

"Stuffy, Gregor, you sound awfully stuffy."

"Yes, sir."

"What you're hinting is that the kind of gentleman I am wouldn't do that."

"It's the more artistic, more bohemian style of gentleman who will wear a turtleneck. It's the theatrical style of gentleman who has ruffles, or a pastel shirt." I put the link through the French cuffs on his right wrist, then moved behind him to do the left.

"You mean the crass style, don't you? Or gay—gays go in for color and ruffles. But I forgot, you don't like that word."

I passed him his trousers. "It's cost us at the least one good line of poetry."

He stepped into the pants, pulled them up, zipped and buttoned them. "Don't be too stuffy, Gregor."

"As you wish, sir."

His reflection grinned at me. I passed him the cummerbund, black of course.

"Do you know anything about this opera? *Marriage of Figaro*? It's Mozart, right? I'm not a complete dunce, I know that much."

I put his evening shoes down by his feet.

"Is there something interesting I could say about it, so I don't come across as a complete jerk? Pruny has cultural interests—" He ran a little finger along a mocking eyebrow. "I don't want to give her false hope, but I do have my pride. Do you know anything about it?"

"There's the point of the connotations in the title."

He waited for me to go on. I held the tie ready. He turned his back to the mirror and I put the tie behind his neck. "Well?" he asked. "Are you going to tell me?"

"The title in Italian, *Le Nozze di Figaro...*" I gave each syllable Italianate values, apple-plump vowels, a savoring of the double *z* and an embellishment of the *r*.

He tried to do the same, a pale imitation.

"*Nozze*," I told him, "isn't only the nuptials, the marriage ceremony, it's...the wedding night, something like that, and it's plural, whatever you want to make of that."

"And?" He was impatient now. "What do I make out of that? A wedding night only matters that way if everyone's a virgin—no, if the girl is. Which sounds pretty chancy as a conversation piece, virginity. Pruny'd probably faint. Or blush. Or something."

"There's the pastoral tradition," I offered, stepping back to be sure that the tie was perfectly even.

Mr. Theo groaned. "Do you mean there are going to be shepherds and shepherdesses doddling around on the stage?" I laughed. "I don't think I can take that," he said, and seemed sincere.

"Pastoral more in the music than the drama," I promised him. We were grinning at one another in the mirror. "You could talk about the role of women."

"Now that sounds more like it. You don't have to know anything to talk about that. You just say something like"— he slipped his arms into the jacket—"'Interesting what he does with the role of women in the world of the play.' I remember that trick from freshman English; I can do that. You sound smart without having to actually know anything. Don't look at me like that, Gregor. I know my limits."

He studied himself in the mirror. I turned to take the dress overcoat from its hanger.

"I should take you with me to a business lunch someday, let you see me in my element, teach you a little respect and admiration."

It wasn't an invitation. If it had been, I would have declined it.

"Do you want me to drive tonight?"

"Why should both of us be bored?" He looked at his watch. "The garage said they'd have the car here by seven thirty; it's about time. You know, if we were identical, I could send you in my place. You'd probably enjoy it."

"I probably would." I held out his coat.

"And I'm just going to spend the next several hours feeling inadequate. Do you know what we do these weekends, when they leave us alone? They do that, with dismal regularity, they think they're being so subtle. They yawn, 'If you two young people don't mind…' Prune huddles in her chair, then asks if I'd like a game of Scrabble. Scrabble, I ask you, Gregor—and she always beats me too."

I passed him the car keys, a white silk scarf, gloves.

"They'll give up soon, and she's not offensive, which is something. She's not ugly and she's quiet. It's no trouble, she's no trouble. *And* my parents are leaving, day after tomorrow, for a whole month. Well"—a final lingering glance in the mirror—"if I don't get going we'll miss the beginning. Women's role, right? At least it's timely. It always looks good to be timely."

I watched him leave the room. "Enjoy your evening, sir."

He turned at the door, careless, carefree, dashing. He seemed the kind of man who would joke on his way up the gallows steps, a good man to die beside, gallant, or fight beside; but a bad man for a night at the opera or a humdrum life. His eyes lingered on the mirror, briefly.

13

FORTUNE SMILES

I was vacuuming the downstairs, cleaning up after Friday evening in preparation for what Saturday might bring. I had gotten to the library when Mr. Theo surprised me by coming in.

The woman with him was no surprise—I mean, that he had a woman with him. They had apparently met at the Racquet Club: they carried identical satchels, with handles emergent, and they wore identical Nikes, and they looked identically well-exercised, somewhere between sweaty and aglow. I turned off the vacuum, unplugged it, wrapped the cord around the handle. "I'm finished in here, sir. May I prepare lunch for you and the young lady?"

Mr. Theo was rooting among the letters and invitations on his desk. "No thanks, Gregor. There's champagne on ice, isn't there?" I didn't bother to answer; he knew there was.

"But I have a favor to ask," he said. He'd found what he was looking for.

"Sir?" I attended, vacuum at hand.

He held out an invitation card. "This Jordan Bradshaw, I went to school with him and his family lives out in Connecticut."

The gallery address was downtown, in SoHo. The date—March thirty-first—was that day's.

"I'd like you to go to this opening. I ought to know something in case I run into them, or him. So I'll have some idea of something to say, in case. I can't go myself because we need a shower"—he smiled at the woman—"or two showers, whatever, before we think about anything else. There's a guest room, with a bathroom you can use, Clarisse. Turn left at the head of the stairs."

"I won't be long," she promised, and left the room.

"But change first," Mr. Theo said to me, "into something…less workaday."

He didn't need to remind me. "Do you want me to purchase one of the pictures?"

"Good God, no, man. Friendship is one thing, but money's another. Don't hurry back. Take the afternoon off, see a movie, go to a museum, whatever you like."

"Yes, sir," I said, obtuse. "Will there be two for dinner?"

He was impatient to have me gone, which is why I delayed.

"Forget about dinner. We'll pick up something and then go on to Kyle's. You might eat out yourself, for a change."

He pulled out his wallet, but I shook my head. "Thank you, sir," I said, and left the room, irritated. Irritated also at being irritated. I thought I had my own goal clear in my own mind. I thought I understood Mr. Theo's role in my plan. So why should I be irritated when he behaved like himself? I exited the room, vacuum at my side, like a sport satchel with the long hose emergent.

The taxi let me out at Fifth and Twelfth. A walk would clear my head. Peevish, that's what I'd been. I would, I thought, walk along and give myself a talking to.

But the day was so gently fine that all I could do was savor it, the soft, moist, sunlit air, the puddles on street and sidewalks. A predawn rain had washed the city clean and the mild spring sun hadn't diminished that good effect. People were smiling, as if it were a holiday. Over Washington Square, clouds still gray with rain moved across a hyacinth sky. Contentment flowed into me—illusory, perhaps, probably, ephemeral for sure, but unquestionably present. I crossed Houston. The afternoon was developing a sense of spaciousness and my spirits rose to the occasion.

The gallery was one of several small shops along a two-block stretch, each a single room behind a storefront window. A bell over the door announced me.

Pictures crowded the walls. A couple of women moved in front of them, as smoothly as if they rode a conveyor belt, talking. A man of about my age sat behind a card table, where a hot plate held two full coffeepots and a plastic tray held paper cups, popsicle sticks, sugar packets, and a bottle of nondairy creamer. The man looked at me furtively; I studied him at leisure—an ordinary man, in jeans and tennis shoes, brown work shirt, brown crew-necked sweater, brown Harris tweed jacket. His hair was thinnish, his eyes bluish, his chin weakish; he wore a wedding ring—an ordinary man, probably a nice man, probably also the artist himself. However they are supposed to look, however they think of themselves as looking, artists have the same luck of the draw in their flesh as the rest of us. Talent is not made visible, after all, whatever talents a man has. Or a woman. This man was seated where the gallery owner or artist would be, and thus was one or the other. I guessed the artist, because nobody who hoped to turn a profit would wear such a rabbity expression.

My smile was unnecessary, so I turned to the exhibit. The hodgepodge effect on the walls required me to mentally isolate each picture from the others, and I concentrated on that. Watercolor. Landscapes with an occasional house or church or street inconsequential to the shape of the earth beneath and its overlay of grass, bush, trees. The events of the sky. Gardens in flower, sometimes with a doorway or gate to one side. I was interested: he achieved an intensity of color with the watercolors that had almost the depth of oils, like Winslow Homer's Key West paintings. He was worth looking at, this Jordan Bradshaw. Even three winter scenes, although outnumbered by the more picturesque seasons, were done with the same intense palette, a whiteness as heavy as snow.

The women left with a jingle of the bell and I began a slow, solitary, second circuit. If I had attended to it, I would have felt the man's eyes, like a finger poking at my back or ribs; but the longer I looked, the less could I be distracted from the pictures. The bell over the door rang and I glanced over.

It was her.

I turned my back quickly. The man's chair scraped, his feet hurried. I heard her voice. "Hello, Jordan."

I was completely unready. I felt as if I had fallen into icy water. It tasted like fear, like sudden danger.

"Don't look so surprised. I told you I'd come," she said.

All of my plans and hopes, lost. I wondered if I could leave without being noticed, if she had noticed me.

"Alexis," the man said. "Oh Alexis, I'm so glad to see you."

I took a deep breath. Nothing was lost, necessarily. Nothing was out of control. I was being a fool.

"I came right from class," Alexis soothed him.

I blew my breath out softly. It was an accident, a lucky chance. It was nothing to do with me. Except to take up the chance.

"How about some coffee? Stay there, I'll get it—black? Don't look around yet."

I turned then, while his back was to the room, and she saw me. Her instinctive smile—ordinary courtesy for a familiar face—faltered into surprise, then pleasure, then dismay. I went over to her. "Don't disappear," I asked her. Before she could decide, I hurried on to explain, "Right now, he seems to need your attentions."

"Yes," Alexis said.

I was across the room before I understood that she could have been agreeing to anything. It was too late to ask for clarification so I kept my eyes on the paintings.

"Take it, before I spill it." His voice was low, and if I hadn't been listening I needn't have overheard them. "Don't ask me to walk you around and talk about what I mean by it all. You'd think Chris would know by now how useless I am, but he said I had to be here for the opening. He'll be in soon, so—And the last show we did here sold out, but you can't be sure, you can't count on it, you don't know how much is just people hoping to get on a bandwagon early. They just rush through, something to do before lunch. They don't even stop talking, it's like being the pianist at a bar. Except that man, him, he's really looking, so it doesn't matter if he buys. He has a look to him, do you think? A professional gambler, or maybe CIA? Syndicate lawyer? Or the movies. Probably he's meeting someone and drifted in to kill time."

"Slow down, Jordan." There was laughter in her voice. "You're making me anxious just standing next to you."

"I'm sorry," he said, miserable.

"It's only a show. It's working that matters, you've told me that."

There was a hesitation. I studied the shadow of a tree on a snowy slope.

"You're right," Jordan said, and he sounded calmer. "You're absolutely right."

I almost turned around at the sound of his voice: like a man who has been kissed to discovery.

"You know," Alexis said, "what I really want to do is come back when you're not here. So I can look at what you've been doing without having you…"

"Sniveling in your ear?" he suggested.

"If I do that, would you mind?"

But she'd given me her word. At least she had let me think she was giving it.

"Of course not. It can't be pleasant to have me hanging over your shoulder."

"I'll call you."

"Panting for praise."

I turned around at the bell. She was going out the door, walking away. Outside, she stopped herself. I turned back to the pictures.

The bell rang again. "I'm just going to walk around once. Quickly. Please ignore me, Jordan."

Time, I didn't have enough time to think how to do it right. "Alexis," I greeted her, my voice low, private. "It's a lovely name for you, Alexis."

"How did you know I'd be here?" She spoke as softly as I did but it still felt as if she'd shouldered me out of her way.

I stumbled for balance. "I had no idea. How could I know that?"

"I'm not sure I can believe what you say."

I gave her a minute to think that over.

"I'm sorry," she whispered. "I do know I can believe you."

I didn't say anything.

"Poor Jordan," she said. "He'd be much happier if he could live on top of some mountain and just send paintings down by mule as he finished them, and never—I *said* I was sorry."

Then I looked down into her face, not trying to conceal my pleasure at seeing her. "You don't have to apologize."

"You have to admit it's—"

I interrupted, still speaking softly, feeling the awkwardness of attempting subtle courtship at a whisper. "I'd like to take you to lunch."

"I can't. No, that's not true. But I'm not hungry."

This was the moment of choice, for both of us. I decided to risk it. Others, I'd gotten no further than two or three meetings with; Alexis was also the first I'd tracked to her home. But I didn't know how she would react if I pressed the matter, if I refused to accept her excuse, so I took a compromising position. "Then let's walk back uptown. It's a beautiful day and maybe you'll get hungry."

"I can't," she said quickly. "Well, no, yes, I could. And I am hungry, that wasn't true. All right, I will, I'd like to. Have lunch," she specified. "With you."

"Shall I wait for you outside?" I offered. I could afford to be generous.

"Why?"

"Your friend Jordan—"

"Oh, Jordan." She'd forgotten him. But at that moment four other people entered the gallery and Jordan didn't even say good-bye to her.

I knew I didn't dare let it go to my head, that whiff of victory, possibility coming a step closer—a seven-league boot step closer—but I had to let it go to my head, for just a minute. The street and everyone on it, and everything on it, seemed to sparkle. Even the grime sparkled. I couldn't think of anything to say and neither did she. I hoped I looked the way I wanted to, not the way I felt.

Before the silence could change from companionable to uncomfortable, I found a restaurant that looked right, white tablecloths and fresh flowers. We were seated, we were given menus. She studied hers and I studied her face.

I had no idea what she might be thinking. While we learn ourselves from the inside out, learn to recognize and then know ourselves, we learn others from the outside in. I knew too little about Alexis. Her hair shone, and she wore a pale heather suit over a pale green sweater. She looked dumpy, there was no way around it. Expensive, but dumpy. Her cheeks were flushed, just a little, and I couldn't guess what that meant. She looked up then. I smiled, an attempt at reassurance. She smiled back uneasily. Her light brown irises were ringed with a black band: candid eyes.

"Let's just relax and—" I said, at the same time that she spoke, "I think I'm glad you—"

We both fell silent.

"Go ahead."

"No, you."

We turned to the waiter with relief. I had ice water; Alexis asked for lemonade.

Another silence.

I didn't dare end it with the wrong words: a line had been crossed, after which things couldn't be the same. She had crossed a line she'd drawn. Or, I corrected myself, I had pulled her over it. I knew too little about her, which was a serious impediment. That she could be persuaded I knew, by someone whose will was stubborn; I thought she would always give way to persistence. That she was oddly immature, and she dressed without any sense of style, without any style of her own. That she felt insufficient to the world she lived in, ill at ease in it. That there was money, real money.

"Your friend Jordan is good, isn't he?" I chose to say.

"I think so," and she smiled in pleasure for her friend. So she was a nice person, that too. Which would work to my advantage. "Unusual," she added.

"Unusual?" I thought of his entirely ordinary appearance, and entirely traditional subjects, and wondered how flat and gray the usual she spoke of might be; then I remembered his depth of color and a curious—now that I thought of it—lack of human life in his work. "How so?" I thought I knew what she would answer, but I was wrong.

"People like us, especially if they're talented, don't usually fulfill their promise," she explained. When she wasn't conscious of herself, her face became expressive, and even attractive—in the sense that it attracted the eye and pleased it. She would never turn heads and she wasn't what you'd call pretty, but she could be the kind of woman you would look at and think, *I'd like to know her.*

"People like us?" I asked, hoping to find out what she thought of me.

"You know what I mean, like you and me." She hesitated. "The leisure class."

"What does that mean?"

I should have said, What do *you* mean by that? but it was too late to change my words.

"You must have taken a sociology course."

"I never went to college."

That stopped her. "Oh." And puzzled her, although she didn't ask me about it. "Then," and she said it kindly, lest she give offense, the danger of giving offense outweighing any interest in taking offense, "It means people like me, my parents, Jordan—and you too. You do a man of mystery act, but you strike me as the same. Different, but the same too." She was looking at me; I don't know what she saw. My guess was that part of my appeal for her was that sense of mystery. I was wary, alert: it would be stupid to underestimate her intelligence. "I think," she added, doubting her opinion as soon as she'd uttered it.

She went on, almost as if having started a process of thought, she couldn't stop it. "Ordinary rich people, or not-extraordinary rich people. Inherited, you know, money. It's a handicap, in its way, money, if you think about it. I think there should be special parking places, marked with dollar signs on them, no, don't laugh, I'm serious. Sometimes I think I'd like to run away and be nobody so I could be somebody." She heard her own words and smiled, ruefully; she leaned back again. Wanting me to understand, she had put her elbows on the table and leaned toward me. "But I can't."

"Why not?" I knew I should ask something else, talk about something else—maybe take up the proffered topic of money in the abstract, to engage her mind, or go back to Jordan to engage her sympathy—but I wanted to hear why not.

"Oh, my parents—I'm an only child and…it wouldn't be real anyway, because I'd always know…" She thought about it. "Besides, I'm not sure how I'd do. I'd probably fail. Besides, why should I have to? What's wrong with being who I am?"

I knew the right response. "I like you just the way you are."

She refused to let the conversation settle into an easy canter. "You don't know anything about me."

"Not much," I agreed, "yet."

She picked up her fork. I hadn't even noticed our plates being set before us. "I'm glad you liked Jordan's work." She took herself back to a safe topic. "Are you a collector?"

"Not really. More of an appreciator."

She had nothing to say to that. We had been, briefly, forward and now that was ended. I wasn't sure how to take us forward again. I opted for flattery, which is cheap but usually an effective approach. "I'm really glad I ran into you."

She nodded her head, expressionless.

"It was already a good day, and this makes it perfect."

She didn't quarrel, didn't agree, didn't look at me. Was embarrassed, self-conscious, uncomfortable.

I was losing ground, visibly, but didn't know in what other direction to flail. "Almost like magic"—floundering glibly—"in answer to a wish—"

Her glance stopped me, like a slap across the face. She was cross, bored and cross, and ashamed. I didn't blame her. Neither did I blame myself: she wasn't giving me much help in elevating the conversation. But then, I had much more invested in the success of this lunch than she did.

"You don't believe in fairy tales," I remarked, drawing back into safety, hoping to pass my stupidity off as attempted wit.

"Oh, I might believe in *them*," she said.

She didn't need to say what she didn't believe in.

She said it anyway. "It's you I'm having trouble believing in."

It was a moderately humiliating moment, a difficult moment to seem blind to. The only consolation I could offer myself was that this was a personal reaction. If she hadn't previously thought well of me, I couldn't have disappointed her, I told myself. I wasn't much comforted, sitting stiff and wondering if I had to let her insult me, if that was a necessary part of the arrangement. "Maybe because I'm not a fairy tale," I said, having reached a quarrelsome state myself.

"You can't be, you're a real person. Fairy tales have to be apart from reality, distant—" Her whiskey eyes, within their dark rims, looked beyond me as if she had recognized someone in the street. Her smile was unselfconscious, for herself, not for me. "That's what's wrong with *Into the Woods*," she announced. "I just figured it out."

I had started to turn around to see who it was, and I halted. "You mean the second act?"

"Because he forced a modern reality into a fairy-tale world. You've seen it?"

I'd seen it, with an empty seat beside me. "Yes," I said.

"Didn't that time when everyone was going to turn Jack over to the giant's wife and save their own skins—everybody trying to save themselves, and only the common man had *nous,* and there's no heroism and no hope for heroism."

I knew I should draw her out and be curious about what interested her, but that isn't what I did. "Twentieth-century cynicism is really only moral relativism. That's why the first act did work."

She hadn't followed me. I admit to being pleased at finding myself a step ahead.

"Because it was purely comic, just a switched point of view."

"A tale told by an *enfant terrible*," she said, smiling.

"Nasty," I said. If I thought, I'd have held my tongue. I did neither. "You have a nasty streak."

She waved that problem away, happy, eager. Alexis shook out her mind like some women shake out their hair, to display its bright tumbling qualities, to attract. "Real fairy tales are pretty cynical."

"Cruel, yes, but I don't see cynical."

She dropped Bettelheim on me—Red Riding Hood as learning the difference between the seductive, devouring wolf-man and the protective, well-socialized hunger-man. I listened politely, awaiting my chance to drop Freud on her—Red Riding Hood's little red cloak the symbol of menstruation and the dangers of sexual maturity. She kicked Freud aside and suggested a Jungian archetype. We had a fine time. I let Alexis do most of the talking, and I didn't have to fake my interest. Most women are less reluctant to show you their breasts than their minds, and I may know why. Alexis had no such qualms of modesty, or if she had, she had forgotten them in the pleasure of conversation.

"Especially cynical about women," she finally said. "Think. I mean *think*." As if I hadn't been doing so. "All a girl has to be is beautiful, although being a princess helps a lot. Snow White's prince doesn't even care if she's dead. Maybe he prefers it. As far as he knows, she *is* dead, and that doesn't make any difference to him, he falls in love with her anyway. Don't you think that's cynical?"

"What are you, a militant feminist?"

"No," she said, "an economics major." She laughed then, with a lifting gesture of her chin, enjoying her own mischief. After a hesitation, to decide something, she told me, "I've got a doctorate, with a specialty in the economics of developing nations."

"Were you teaching the course you told Jordan you came from?"

"No, that's a language course. I'm taking it."

"Spanish?" Her face told me I was right. "You already have French," I guessed again. "You're intelligent," I said, adding to myself, *and rich and unmarried.* "But why economics?"

"I thought, you should understand what you have."

It took me a minute. There was a practicality to the idea, although it wasn't immediately apparent. "So if you'd been beautiful? You'd have—what? Gone to modeling school? Studied aesthetics?"

Then I heard what I'd said.

And Alexis burst out laughing, a warm, chuckling laugh. I could have leaned across the table and kissed her for that laughter. I didn't, of course, that would have been going too far. Instead I looked down, to notice that my plate was empty. I had apparently eaten my lunch. "Dessert? Coffee?"

"I have to go. No, I really do."

"I thought we might walk uptown," I offered.

"I'd like that, but I really can't." She meant both statements and I took her at her word. I was satisfied with my luck, and the use I'd made of it. No need to push it.

I settled the bill and we went back outside. There was too little time before a cab appeared. I held the door open. She hesitated, not getting in. "What *is* your name?" she asked me.

"Gregor." I think I kept my voice calm. Resonant, perhaps, but mostly calm.

Mocking herself, she held out her hand. "How do you do, Gregor. It's a pleasure to meet you."

I let go of the door handle and took her hand. "How do you do, Alexis." Then we were kissing, I have no idea how: we were already doing it before I'd noticed, until she stepped back, into the cab, and away.

I couldn't move. I tried to remember the expression on her face—surprise, a little fear too, fear was part of it; it was definitely a mixed facial response I remembered. It was just a kiss, just lips. I wasn't plummeted into irresistible desire. More to the point, neither was she. It was just a mutual impulse. Her mouth tasted sweet, like the air.

I tried to think clearly, while memory was fresh. It wasn't an experienced kiss and not one she'd anticipated or maneuvered. I didn't know if I'd bent down or if she'd raised her face. We were shaking hands and then kissing; whatever time had separated the events was lost. I was just as surprised as she was. But I wasn't afraid. Or not afraid of the kiss and what it might mean.

14

ENTER SARAH MONDLEIGH

Eagerness, like happiness, is dangerous. So the next morning I took a long, meditative walk—the wrong move now could cost me the prize—and picked up the Sunday *Times* on the way home. As I came down the street I saw a figure seated on Mr. Theo's stoop. Dark-haired, female, two large suitcases at her side.

For two steps my heart was in my throat, and then the unlikelihood of it reached me. I slowed down. She could have no idea of where I lived. Her hair was longer, chin-length, and not so dark. She was a deliberative character, Alexis, not the kind of woman to appear on a man's door-step with suitcases, after a single kiss. She allowed other people to make decisions and for herself decided only whether or not she would go along with them. We were nowhere near the point where she might fly to me; we were barely past the point where she would fly from me. Reason reasserted itself.

The girl did no more than glance at me as I came near. She wore basic urban black—long skirt and long-sleeved T, high-topped shoes—her dark hair swung down to touch her cheekbones, and I wondered, with an anticipation that wasn't entirely unsympathetic, what crisis Mr. Theo had at hand.

I came to a halt before her, the keys in my hand. She looked up at me and smiled—a bright red slash of color. She stood up, a slight thing, a little thing. "You've got to be Gregor, I bet. Are you?"

I nodded. She was young for Mr. Theo, perhaps twenty, and she had those suitcases, which boded ill.

"I'm Theo's little sister. I'm Sarah." She was enjoying my surprise. She was entirely pleased with herself.

"Ah," I said. It made sense when I looked at her. I could see a resemblance. Mr. Mondleigh's domineering genes had been at work here, too—the broad cheekbones, the willful mouth. "How do you do, Miss Sarah. Is Mr. Theo expecting you?"

She was blocking the door, standing between her suitcases. I waited, with a bag of fruit and the *Times*.

"Nobody's expecting me. I've just"—she threw her arms out—"flown away home. You're not at all what I expected. I expected someone stodgy. Old."

I shifted my grip on the bag. "Your parents don't know you've returned?"

"I hope not. I waited until they'd gone south. I'm not in any hurry to hear what they have to say to me. Can't we go in?"

I reached around to unlock the door and hold it for her. I unlocked the inner door and quickly punched the code into the alarm. She stood in the hallway, looking about her, smiling to herself.

I took my parcels into the kitchen.

She wandered into the living room, into the library.

I went back outside to bring in her suitcases. She came out to look expectantly at me. "Shall I take these up to the guest room?" I asked.

"Theo won't mind, will he? I couldn't take it any longer." She ran fingers through her short hair, to express how desperate she had been. "I just couldn't take it any longer, I really couldn't. I need a shower too; I caught a midnight flight."

"If you'll follow me, miss?"

In the guest room I took the luggage racks out of the closet and set the suitcases down on them. She wandered into the bathroom, wandered back.

"When will Theo be home?"

"I'm not sure I expect him tonight."

She smiled knowingly, then giggled. "Same old Theo. I don't want to go out to the Farm, Gregor. Nobody's there."

"I'm sure your brother would want you to stay, miss," I assured her, mendaciously. Mr. Theo would have to straighten this out when he got back. My proper role was to keep an eye on her, keep her safe, until he could take over.

"First, I'll take a long hot shower. Then I'm going to launder my things." She smiled proudly at me. "I'm going to do my own laundry, Gregor."

• • •

I set the table, started a dinner, and considered my options. The best seemed to be a show at the Metropolitan, three centuries of Dutch paintings, landscapes, still lifes, interiors. I cut out the notice, underlined it, and wrote with a ballpoint pen *Sunday, two p.m., Main Entrance.* Miss Sarah interrupted me, entering from the dining room with the placemat, napkin, silver, and glassware in her hands.

"I won't do it." She put the items down on the kitchen table, pushing the *Times* aside.

I rescued my clipping, folded up the Arts section.

"I'm not going to eat alone out there while you eat in here. As if there was something wrong with us sharing a table." She folded the napkin in place, arranged silverware. "That finishing school about finished me, Gregor."

I didn't attempt to argue proprieties. I sat down again, to put my clipping into an envelope, seal it, address it. *Alexis.*

"Have you run away then, miss?" I asked, putting the envelope into my jacket pocket.

"And you calling me Miss Sarah, like something out of *Gone with the Wind.* That kind of stuff has gone with the wind, Gregor."

"It goes against all my training."

"It might be good for you to go against all your training. I have, I am, and I feel so…free and…strong, and everything. What are you doing?" She had sat down. I had arisen. "Where are you going?"

"To get my own plate and serve the meal."

While we ate, she told me about the school, with its boring classes, shallow students, and snobbish faculty, the tedious culture weekends, the hypocrisy of the entire endeavor. "They say you learn French, but everyone speaks English because it's the only common language. It *was* beautiful, a château, right on the river, that part at least was true, but…being beautiful isn't enough. Not for me, anyway."

"Ah." I nodded, which had been all the conversation required from me throughout. As far as I could tell, Miss Sarah meant no harm, and that was good enough for me.

She placed her knife and fork at twenty after two on her plate. I rose to clear. "That wasn't so bad, was it Gregor?"

"Very nice, miss," I said. "Will you have dessert? Coffee?"

"Coffee but no dessert, thanks. You're a really good cook."

I thanked her. She suited my mood, Sarah Mondleigh did: it was like having a kitten in the room, like a vote for unreason.

She studied me over the top of her cup and finally said what she was thinking. "What's someone as young as you doing being a butler anyway? Didn't you want to do something else? Not now, but ever before? Because you're good-looking too, in a handsome way. Didn't you? You must have."

"Yes."

"What?"

"It's none of your business, if I may say so, miss."

Her attention went back to the more interesting subject. "I'd like to stay here for a long visit. If Theo will let me, I'm going to. He'll let me, won't he?"

"I couldn't say."

"And he'll have to call the school to tell them I'm here,

safe. Or you could but you'd have to pretend to be Theo."
I shook my head. "Or I suppose I could, but that wouldn't
convince them because I could be calling from anywhere
and lying about it. Where *is* Theo?"

I couldn't tell her.

"Mother says he might be getting married. Is he?"

"You'll have to ask him."

"But he couldn't be out with Pruny because then he
wouldn't be staying out all night. In by midnight, I bet,
that's what she'd do, maybe one kiss, at the door. Certainly
no sex. No overnights. So he can't be getting married, can
he?" She waited.

"I couldn't say, miss."

"So discreet, so perfectly discreet."

"As you say," I agreed.

She put her cup down impatiently. "Isn't this—all this,
and yourself too—don't you find it awfully dreary?"

"No, miss, I don't," I said, stuffily. She laughed, pleased
with me and herself. It was entirely true, however stuffy:
at that moment, with the envelope in my pocket and the
chance of Alexis, life seemed the opposite of dreary. Life
seemed filled with promises approaching fulfillment.

"Well I do," Miss Sarah announced. "I want things
different, I want to do my own laundry, and I want to do
everything completely differently from the way everybody
always has, different and better. I'm going to do the dishes,
Gregor. No, you can't stop me, I'm serious about this. And
my own ironing too. And, and..." Imagination failed her.
"And everything."

15

ALL FOOLS' DAY

I was preparing a sauce for the pork loin, stirring Madeira into simmering cream; Miss Sarah was ironing, apparently quite happily, chattering about her former roommates; the carrots were ready to go into the steamer; the pilaf—done Middle Eastern style, with almonds and raisins—was cooking in the second oven. Mr. Theo would be home at any moment, and I wondered what he would say to his sister's presence. I found her companionable, no more wrong-headed than any other person her age, and almost painfully sincere.

"This is fun, Gregor." She was working the iron around lacy flounces of a nightgown. "I don't know why women complain about ironing. Everything looks so much nicer after you've ironed it." She looked up from her labors. "You still think I should call Theo."

I'd given up that argument in the early afternoon. She hadn't.

"But what's the difference? He'll know when he gets home, and that won't be long now. It'll be soon enough then. It's his own fault, anyway: he could have come home last night and then he'd already know. If he's going to go tomcatting around…He can't be seriously thinking of getting married; he couldn't be. The parents are going to feel personally let down. He's probably been leading them on, hasn't he? By not seeming to disagree. Although it's what they deserve—trying to make him do what they want him to, not what he wants. Anyway"—she smiled with satisfaction—"he'll be surprised to see me."

I was about to agree when I heard the outer door open. "We'll know in a minute," I told her, removing my apron to go greet Mr. Theo.

She resumed ironing. I considered: should I forewarn Mr. Theo or let Miss Sarah have her surprise? But there were more surprises: the girl with Mr. Theo was young, much too young despite her makeup and a dress that depended on two spaghetti-thin strings to hold it up over bursting breasts. She had the unfinished face of an adolescent. I took a breath, trying to find the right thing to say. He had shocked me. I didn't think he could, or would, but he'd done it.

"Good evening, Gregor."

The girl draped herself over his shoulder. His eyes were bright, his cheeks flushed; his hand rested on her bony hip.

"Good evening. Sir—?"

"Look what followed me home. Do you think I should keep it?"

"Sir?"

"I know, a joke in bad taste." He looked down at her. Her hair had been cut into points, clinging like short pennants around her face; she looked up at him. "Come into my parlor, Carlie."

She giggled.

"We'll slip into the library and have a drink while Gregor sets an extra place. Dinner will feed two, won't it, Gregor?" He gave me no time to answer, only a look of smug sexuality. "Carlie and I seem to be working up quite an appetite."

"I guess we are," she agreed.

"There she was, a gift from the gods. Followed me all the way to the car. If a lady wants to share your limousine, Gregor—"

"Sir. If I could have a word?"

"Now?"

"Just for a moment, sir." My urgency seemed to penetrate his haze of anticipation. "I'm sure the young lady can amuse herself, just for a moment or two."

She draped herself against the doorway, one hand raised to stroke the wood. "Don't be too long." A caricature, an unintentional mockery of every screen seductress—no, every television seductress—she backed into the library. Mr. Theo followed me down the hallway.

"It's incredible what girls will do. God I'm grateful to be alive at this time, to be living in—I've never laid eyes on her before, but she seems to know me. Honestly, I got out of the elevator and she latched herself on to me."

I swung the kitchen door open.

"She knows my name. And what is it that's so important?"

Miss Sarah looked up, iron in her hand, laughter in her eyes. She was, just as she'd hoped, a complete surprise.

"Oh," Mr. Theo said. "Sarah?" He took a couple of steps toward her. "Oh my God, Sarah. What are you doing here? Why aren't you in Geneva or wherever it was?"

She had expected a welcome. She had expected to be a welcome surprise.

"What are you doing? Ironing?"

"It's fun," she said, sulky.

"Well you can't stay here. You've got to go."

She put the iron back on its holder, reached across to pull the plug out of the socket, pulled the nightgown off the ironing board—slow and recriminating gestures.

"No, not right now. I didn't mean—Wait. Wait a minute, let me think. Look, Sarah, just stay out here. OK? Stay in the kitchen and don't come out." He was thinking fast, thought made visible. "If anybody asks you, you're the maid or something. I can't explain, but this is a real problem. You shouldn't be here," he told her.

Miss Sarah folded her arms under her breasts. "Don't worry, I'll go to a hotel. You don't have to worry about me."

"I'm sorry," Mr. Theo said. She didn't accept the apology. She held her chin high and her nose above it. "I didn't mean it, you don't have to leave. Look, I'll explain later. Don't pay any attention to me. Gregor"—he was back in command of the situation—"we'll have dinner right away, the sooner the better, then we'll be out of here."

"*We?*" Miss Sarah metamorphosed into a shrew. "What *we*? You and who, *we*? Not Prune, I bet; for Prune you wouldn't keep me in the kitchen. As the maid. Nothing to say for yourself, Theo?"

"It's none of your business, honey," he said.

When I set dinner plates down before the romantic couple, she had moved her place setting until she was sitting not across from but next to him. She wasn't having to work very hard to recapture his entire attention. I served them Scandinavian style, off a single platter, roast, rice, carrots. They paid no attention to me, as if I were not there, or as if I were invisible, like the castle servants in *Beauty and the Beast*. Only in this version, I thought, as she murmured "Teddy-Weddy" at him, the genders were reversed. Or, I thought, it was *Beast and the Beast*, honors equal. I was the only player true to the original.

The doorbell rang as I was spooning cream sauce over the slices of roast.

The doorbell didn't ring once, then wait for a response. It rang steadily, like an alarm. I set the platter down on the table.

When I opened the street door, I was all pomp and presence at the unmannerly summons, and a dark force went by me, tall, and the shoulders with which he shoved me aside were broad.

"Sir?" I inquired, in a corrective and I hoped warning voice. "What—?"

He was already inside, at the living room door and spinning around to look in the library. He paid no attention to me, gave no more than a dark, angry glance as he ran back toward me, then swung around to thunder up the stairs.

Probably not a thief, I deduced. I didn't follow him.

His footsteps pounded along the upstairs hall. There was the sound of doors, opening, closing. I waited.

He stopped halfway down the staircase to glare at me. "Where are they? I saw them come in. You'll keep out of it if you know what's good for you."

I could almost see the gears of his mind turning, and then, as they meshed, he was on the run again. He shoved my restraining hand aside and went back down the hall. I was on his heels. I didn't know who he was, or what, but I was making a guess. I didn't think there was cause for fear. I could match him; a young man like that wouldn't have learned how to fight in the kind of places where I'd picked up my skills.

We entered the dining room as one. Carlie was feeding Mr. Theo a bite of roast, or perhaps it was a carrot; my memory isn't exact on the point. The young man stopped dead in his tracks and I ran up against his broad back.

Mr. Theo's mouth stayed open. The fork froze in the air. Mr. Theo put his hands against the table to push himself back and up. "What the—?"

"Oh shit," Carlie said. Her fork clattered onto the plate.

"You," the young man said to Mr. Theo, "are a son of a bitch. You," he said to Carlie, in the same growling voice, "get your coat."

I stood back, to watch.

Mr. Theo rose aggressively from his seat. His nostrils flared. "Just one minute here."

The young man moved toward Carlie. "You heard me." She stayed where she was, seated. He turned his attention to Mr. Theo. He came to stand in front of him, looming over him. He shoved Mr. Theo backward, toward the buffet. "You think you can get away with—" Anger choked his voice. "Well you can't, Teddy Mondleigh, not this time. You aren't going to."

At the sound of his own name, Mr. Theo relaxed. "Hey." He pushed the hand away. "Cut it out, will you? Do I know you?"

"You know me." The hand shoved again. Mr. Theo batted it away. "And I know you."

"I said, stop it." The nostrils flared again. Mr. Theo called in his reserves. "Gregor?"

I moved toward the fray, to take the young man into an armlock, I thought. Carlie leaped up and hung onto my arm. She opened her mouth over my wrist.

I restrained myself from slugging her, although if she did bite me I wasn't sure I could answer for my reaction.

But she screamed instead, shrill as a siren.

"Help! Help! Police! Someone!"

She hung off my arm, impeding me.

"Somebody, help!"

The young man ignored us. "Bradley Wycliffe. I was three years behind you at Yale." He had Mr. Theo by the shoulders now and was shaking him. I grabbed Carlie around the waist with my free arm. The young man shook Mr. Theo—"You've already met my sixteen-year-old sister"—shook him hard, to match each syllable.

That news stopped me in my tracks. Mr. Theo's face, even as it flopped back and forth, registered shock.

"My sixteen-year-old sister, Mondleigh." The young man spat the words.

Carlie let go of my arm. "Oh shit," she said.

Mr. Theo regained his composure. He punched at the young man's chest and threw his full weight against him. Mr. Wycliffe stumbled, off balance, and sprawled backward onto the table. Glasses tumbled. Silver scattered. "And *keep* your hands off me, Wycliffe."

Mr. Wycliffe shoved his hands onto the table, to regain his feet. A glass cracked under the pressure. We all fell silent. He lifted his left hand slowly, and by the time he got it up to eye level, blood had begun to flow.

Carlie screamed in earnest.

Blood flowed down his wrist, soaking the buttoned cuff of his white shirt, soaking into the knitted cuff of his Aran Isles sweater.

Carlie screamed again. I let go of her and reached for a napkin, to staunch the flow. Mr. Theo stood panting.

Mr. Wycliffe held his hand out so I could wrap the napkin around it.

The kitchen door flew open and Miss Sarah ran in. "What's happening?"

"Get out of here, Sarah," Mr. Theo panted.

She looked at me. "Should I call the police?" Then she caught sight of the young man. Who was staring at her.

I'd never before seen it happen. They were like two animals that suddenly discover they are sharing space each had thought was his own, a dog and a cat at the moment of realization of each other's presence. "What have you done to him, Theo?" Miss Sarah asked, but her eyes never left the young man's face.

"Who are you?" he asked her, holding the bandage in place with his right hand.

"Just get out of here, both of you," Mr. Theo said.

"I'm the maid."

Carlie was sniffling, weeping, so I picked up another napkin for her, to mop her eyes with and blow her nose into. "Would you like me to call the police, sir?" I inquired.

"No, that won't be necessary. Have you cooled down, Wycliffe?"

There was no answer.

"Sarah, I told you to go back to the kitchen."

She moved toward the door but stayed in the room.

Mr. Wycliffe turned away from her. "Get your coat, Carlie, you little"—he looked back at Miss Sarah—"fool."

His sister pushed her face up at him. "You've ruined everything. I hate you."

"All right, we'll leave the coat."

"The young lady's coat is in the hallway," I said. I was waiting to escort them out.

"But your hand," Miss Sarah said.

"It's just a cut. Not serious," he told her. "Sarah. No, don't," he said, as she reached a hand to take the napkin away, survey the damage. "What's someone like you doing here? Don't try to lie, I've been upstairs. It makes me sick," he told her.

"What do you mean it makes you sick?"

Mr. Theo interrupted. "You did say sixteen? Did you say sixteen?"

Slowly, the young man turned to face his adversary. "Sixteen. As in statutory rape."

"Oh my God." Mr. Theo sank into his chair.

"This one at least looks the age of consent. Barely."

Sarah had understood. "How can you say that? You don't know anything about me."

"What is it then, are you his?" He indicated me by a nod of the head. He couldn't seem to take his eyes away from her face. "Convenient and cozy."

"How about leaving, Wycliffe? Believe it or not, I'm grateful to you, but you've overstayed your welcome. For the record, *she* picked *me* up. Waiting for me, lying in wait, outside the office. For the record."

Mr. Wycliffe paid no attention to him. "And you look as good as gold," he said to Miss Sarah.

"Which is more than can be said for *your* sister," Mr. Theo said.

Those words seemed to sink in. "Carlie, is he telling the truth? Did you do that?"

Carlie was all rebellion. "Of course it's true. What do you think? I'd been waiting half an hour for you. You couldn't be bothered to be on time, what do you expect? I'm sick of boys, and he was in your alumni register. I saw his name. So I did. So what?"

"Oh my God," Mr. Theo groaned.

"But why him?" Mr. Wycliffe asked.

"It's not as if he's married or anything."

The young man kept his temper, barely. "You're going home tomorrow, first plane out."

"Not unless you promise not to tell."

Mr. Theo stood up. "Just get out of my house, will you both?"

"With pleasure," Mr. Wycliffe answered. "Come on, Carlie. I'll never set foot in this"—he looked at Miss Sarah for the last time—"whoremaster's haven again."

I followed them to the door. He had his right hand at

the back of his sister's neck, not gently. He took her coat without thanks. I closed the door behind them.

Miss Sarah was gathering up pieces of glass, mooning over them. Mr. Theo remained seated, except that now his face was buried in his hands. I spread out a clean napkin, to cover the bloodstains.

"Will they come out?" Miss Sarah wondered.

"I know how to remove blood. I had a sister," I told her, I don't know why.

"Sixteen," Mr. Theo mumbled, through his fingers.

"Do you know what he thought?" Miss Sarah asked.

She didn't need to tell me who *he* was. "The gentleman made that fairly clear."

Her outrage needed expression. "He thought I was living here. As in, living with, as in sex. With Theo." She thought. "Or you."

"You have to excuse him. The girl was his sister. He was upset."

Mr. Theo lowered his hands. He spoke to both of us. "I honestly had no idea."

Miss Sarah turned on him. "Look what you've done. With your…womanizing."

"How was I supposed to know?" Mr. Theo asked her. He was happier now that he could justify himself.

"Who is he, Theo?"

"I don't know. I can't remember. Brad Wycliffe, he rowed crew, that's all I remember. From Chicago. Or Iowa. Somewhere out there, it's Wycliffe Industries—grain, beef, I read somewhere they're expanding into fertilizers. He was only a freshman, Sarah. Don't pester me now."

"If I'd been him, I'd have slugged you. You know, he came to rescue her. I bet you wouldn't do that for me."

Mr. Theo wasn't interested in hypothetical situations. "I could have gone to prison. Doesn't that mean anything to you? I'd better get married. I'd better do something about myself."

"If you'll set the table again, Miss Sarah? For two."

She turned on me. "I told you not to call me *miss*." She turned on Mr. Theo. "He thinks I'm your mistress, Theo, or playmate, or whatever. Are you listening to me?"

"Or Gregor's," Mr. Theo said, starting to grin. "Or both of ours."

She was not amused. "How could you do this to me?"

"I'm sorry, really. I sure didn't mean to. I had no idea, and I am sorry. I'm a pretty sorry specimen, all around."

I gathered up the dirty plates. "I'll serve dinner again."

"Don't bother, I don't have much appetite left. That was a sixteen-year-old girl, Gregor." He spoke man to man. "My God—and I had no idea, absolutely no idea. Do you know how much a lawsuit could cost me? A man with my assets?" He shuddered at the thought. "I'm going to give up sex, give up women. Get married."

Miss Sarah stood puffed up with anger. "Lucky Prune."

"If you'll permit me, sir, you'll feel better about things after you've eaten. You'll feel better in the morning."

"No, I mean it," Mr. Theo said. "I'd better. Before I do something serious to myself."

16

PUTTIESQUE FORCES ATTACK

This time there were two of them on the steps, under a fall of April sunshine. Miss Sarah wore jeans and one of those loose sweaters that manages to suggest how succulent is the flesh it conceals. The young man wore slacks and a crew-neck sweater. I wondered how he earned his living, to be so casual in the middle of a Tuesday morning.

Miss Sarah stood up, ostensibly to greet me and offer to take one of the grocery bags I carried. "I've explained everything, Gregor. He knows I'm your sister."

The young man stood.

I wished I could sit down, somewhere solitary, to ingest this piece of information.

He held out a forthright hand and smiled. "Brad Wycliffe."

I shifted the bag, shook his hand.

"I apologize for what I said last night. And thought. Apology accepted?"

"Accepted," I said. Miss Sarah, taking the bag from me, looked urgently into my face.

"Although I still think she shouldn't be living here, in Teddy Mondleigh's house."

"Mr. Mondleigh would never," I assured him.

Miss Sarah stood between us, hugging the grocery bag, beaming from one of us to the other. Brad Wycliffe had three or four inches on me, a lean man, and young. He had an open face, wholesome, the bones squaring it off, a firm mouth, a firm handshake. If she *had* been my sister, he was just the kind of young man I'd have liked her to have taken up with. Four-square, reliable.

"Gregor would poison his soup or something if he tried anything, and he knows it," Miss Sarah said.

"And I also admire the way you've taken care of Sarah, since your parents died," Mr. Wycliffe added.

I didn't dare say anything.

"See? I *have* told him all about us. Even about how I'm studying dance."

"Even about dance? Well, I'm glad that's cleared up."

She smiled happily at me.

"Would you care to come inside?" I asked the young man.

He shook his head, emphatically. "Into Mondleigh's house? Not a chance. I'll pick you up at noon tomorrow, Sarah?"

"Yes." Her cheeks were pink.

"Until tomorrow then," he said. "Gregor," and he shook my hand again.

"See you," she called after him, watching his long

stride, watching until he had turned the corner and moved out of sight.

That scene played out, she let me into the house. As I followed her into the kitchen, I debated whether I should say anything, and if so, what. She put the grocery bag down on the table. I set mine beside it.

"What kind of dance are you studying, miss? In case he asks."

Miss Sarah giggled, did a turn around the room, concluding with a court curtsey at my feet. She raised her head to look at me. "Ballet. We're working here to pay for the lessons. Do you mind?"

A pretty black pot myself, I couldn't scold, but I could warn her. "You'd be wiser to tell him the truth."

"Isn't he wonderful? Did you notice his eyes? And he has a great laugh, but you haven't heard it."

Nothing I said would have gotten through to her.

"He didn't want to come back here," she told me. "He didn't want to see me again. He likes me, but he doesn't want to. At first it was because of what he thought, and now because he thinks I'm not...in his class. But I think that's why he likes me too, because he doesn't want to."

She moved to give me room to work.

"He says Carlie is a real mess, and he's right, she is. I'll tell him the truth when the time is right. Do you think he'll think I'm after his money? I bet he might, and if he still... likes me, in spite of everything..." The vision occupied her for a minute. "I think I'll wear a denim jumper. That's the kind of thing I'd wear, isn't it? I'll have to get one, this afternoon, with a turtleneck and flats. Where does Theo keep his old yearbooks, Gregor?"

17

ON THE STEPS OF
THE METROPOLITAN

I am a hopeful person, I think. Hope doesn't require belief, or even confidence. I hope the world will not explode into annihilation and self-immolation, and I ground that hope in the growth of international economic dependencies, so it seems to me reasonable. On that Sunday afternoon in April, I stood at the top of the steps of the Metropolitan Museum in a windy sunlight, full of hope. But not greedy: I hoped only that she would arrive.

When I saw her getting out of a taxi, I started down. The staircase stretched between us, a descent of shallow steps, impossible to run down. I don't know what I thought would happen if I didn't get to her on time.

She wore a pale, flowery yellow skirt and matching

blouse, more little-girl Liberty prints. She stopped a few steps below me. Her expression gave me warning. "Hello," she said.

"It's good to see you." I was openly eager.

"I almost didn't come."

Despite my effort, she had gone ahead and done it, leaving me no choice but the truth. "I was afraid of that."

"But I decided it wouldn't be right just to stay away. Just not show up."

"I would have wondered," I said. People moved around us but we stayed as we were, with the steps between us. "If I'd gone too far." I gave her the opening.

"I didn't want you to think I'm the kind of girl— woman, person—who is frightened off by reality. Sex. Or whatever. You know, that old cliché, the person who just wants some daydream. Or just to tease. I don't think I am. But I thought I ought to come and say I wasn't going to come." Her hand shaded her eyes. Her skirt snapped against her calves. She had something more to tell me. I didn't know what it would be, so I spoke with unmitigated neutrality. "That was thoughtful of you."

She took a breath. "There's a man, Gregor."

And he wasn't me. The Someone Else had entered the scene, and there was too much I didn't know about her. It never crossed my mind that she might be lying in order to brush me off gently. It took me a while to ask, "Do you love him?"

"I used to." Remembering made her smile, a little ironic lifting of the corners of her mouth.

I tried to understand what she was telling me. That her one true love still burned in her heart so that whatever she had to offer me was ashes from that fire? Or—she had used the past tense—that she was somehow still committed to the man? "Do you love him now?" I asked.

She thought of her answer, thought it over. I thought of what I knew about her: she was truthful, she was compliant.

"I don't know," she said, finally.

That was all I needed to hear. I moved down the steps.

"But it's not as simple as that, you know it's not."

I knew then that she found me as attractive as I hoped.

"What's your last name, Gregor?"

"Rostov."

"Rostov like in *War and Peace*?" That amused her.

"Rostov like in *War and Peace*," I agreed. If she wanted to ask questions, that was a good sign.

"Do you have brothers and sisters?" The wind blew her hair into her eyes and she raised a hand to hold it back.

"I'm one of four children."

"Which one?"

"The youngest." Lest she run out of questions, I gave her information: "I haven't seen any of them for years." Fifteen years, now I thought of it: a long time. An awfully long time, now I thought of it.

"Why not?"

"I left home."

She was gathering information about me. "So you're a self-made man," she concluded.

"Yes."

There was a long pause.

"I don't know what to say," she said.

"I don't think expressions of sympathy are in order."

And she smiled. "No." The smile faded. "I know it

sounds dumb but—I know I'm naive, and a cliché and—You aren't a criminal of some kind, are you? I'm serious."

I stopped laughing. "I'm not. Honestly."

"Because I'm not very good at judging people. I live a fairly narrow life, and I'm never sure of my opinions. Or sure of myself, for that matter." This worried her. "I sometimes think that's why I keep going to school, because as long as I'm in school I don't have to…But even there I'm not sure. I'm not so sure I'm smart enough. It could be just because of who my family is. Schools do that, hoping for bequests, and I don't blame them. Everybody does it."

I couldn't, in conscience, argue the point.

"So I never know…"

It was time for me to make it easy for her. "You're not married, are you?"

"No." A quick answer for a silly question.

"Well then, we could go see this exhibit." I gave her a little time to follow the *non sequitur* backwards. "Or," I offered, "if I make you uncomfortable, you could go home." I looked into her face. "I do like the way you lift your chin when you laugh, Alexis."

She was relaxed again and would fall in with my plans. "I'm not uncomfortable with you," she said.

Whatever the crisis was, I'd maneuvered her past it. "Then, after, we could have dinner and—I've been wondering what it would be like to dance with you."

The wind pulled at her blouse. "I can't—"

I interrupted her. "Not a disco," I promised. "But foxtrots, and anything else based on the box step. Remember the box step? We might go as far as a waltz."

I put my hand out to her, a gesture she could ignore

if she wished to. She took my hand. "Yes," she said to me. "I'd like that. Yes."

We went back up the steps together, hands clasped. I didn't mind if there was another man. I was looking for marriage, not love.

18

ROMEO AND JULIET

I had Alexis on my mind. I thought I understood how she saw me, what I was in her life. I needed to negotiate the merger of romance with marriage, and I didn't kid myself that it would be easy. She did find me attractive; in my manhood, I attracted her. We talked easily; I could make her laugh; there was a savoring quality to her good-night kisses. If she would love me, it would go forward without a hitch, I thought.

Love is the point where a woman balks. For a woman, marriage is a natural step after love, so she quite wisely hesitates at love. At this stage, everything I didn't know about Alexis could make me ineffective, or could lead me into an error that would enable her to step back, clear of love, to step clear of me. I feared risking the error but also feared not seizing the chance.

I was debating this, once again, as I returned home with the ingredients for a *coq au vin*. Miss Sarah and her boyfriend occupied the stoop, where they seemed to have taken up permanent residence. This time, paper bags and plastic wrappers revealed a picnic lunch—eaten one-handed, since he seemed to have welded his right hand to her left. Miss Sarah slid even closer to Mr. Wycliffe to give me passage. "Hi, Gregor."

She had the look. They both had it. They were aglow with happiness.

The young man stood up, brushing crumbs from his sweater. "Hello, Greg."

Reluctantly, I was glad to see them so happy. I couldn't imagine myself ever having looked so young and happy, even though I knew I had. I gave them fully half my attention. "I see you've eaten."

"Brad has something he wants to ask you." Miss Sarah couldn't take her eyes off the young man.

"Yes," he said. He reached down a hand to grasp hers again. "Yes. In point of fact, I want to marry your sister."

That got my attention. "Mi—?" I stopped myself. "Sarah?"

"She's the only sister you have, so I guess it must be her," he said, and then laughed at his own humor.

"I guess it must," I agreed. "Is this what you want to do?" I asked her.

"Oh, yes."

I tried for wordless communication but she was unavailable, as if she believed in the fictional role she had herself created. What could I say to them? It wasn't my place to say anything. "I don't know what to say."

"Your blessing is what we'd like. You're not going to forbid it?" Mr. Wycliffe at least noticed the expression on my face.

"It's all so sudden."

"It doesn't feel sudden to me," he said. He thought he understood my hesitation and spoke from the heart, sincerity personified. "It feels to me as if I've known Sarah all my life, but I lost her. And now I've found her again."

"Oh," Miss Sarah breathed.

I myself had nothing to say.

"And I want to marry her," he declared.

"I don't know what Mr. Mondleigh would think." I was asking her for help.

"What business is it of his?" Mr. Wycliffe asked.

"You know I'm twenty," Miss Sarah reminded me.

"And don't need anyone's consent, is that it?" I stood thinking. Both watched me. "Well," I said, deciding there was no harm in it, "you met, you fell in love, Brad proposed and you said yes, so now you're engaged. I think I can give my blessing to that."

"You sound pretty darned cool about it," the young man said.

"Gregor," Miss Sarah said, and she was the cool one if he'd only known, "we don't mean getting engaged, we mean getting married."

"Getting married?" There was no need to involve me. She might well be costing me my job, which didn't seem to concern her.

"In Maryland," she explained.

"We'll have a honeymoon sometime later. I've taken so many vacation days this week—I couldn't have concentrated anyway, but—We'll be living at my place," Mr. Wycliffe explained.

"Getting married today?"

"Tomorrow, actually."

"It seemed like the best way to celebrate our first anniversary," he told me, as soppy as she was.

"First anniversary?"

"It's a week today that we met," he said.

"What about your family?" I asked him.

"They'll love Sarah. How could they not?"

I didn't love her.

"I'm going upstairs, to pack," Miss Sarah said, gathering up the remains of the picnic. She ran away, up the stairs and into the house, abandoning us together. I don't know how she knew that I wouldn't give her away.

"I can understand your concern," Mr. Wycliffe said to me.

I clutched the grocery bag to my chest. "Can you?"

"Of course. But it's all right, Gregor. My family is Wycliffe Industries. So she'll be well taken care of, I can promise you. She'll never want for anything." I could only nod my head dumbly. "Greg, I never believed in love like this, just hitting you over the head and knocking you out. But now it's happened to me, and—"

I cut the rhapsody short. "Would you think of waiting a little?"

"I won't change my mind."

"Your family might well object, and I can understand why they would."

"Don't you see? That's why a *fait accompli* is the best way. Then they'll have to band together, for the sake of the family, for family honor. They might be difficult, a little, at first. I won't try to kid you about that, Greg. But I'm not worried. I promise you, I'm no Teddy Mondleigh. I don't sleep around like he does. I've had only two serious relationships in my life, and this isn't like either of them. With Sarah it's different. If I'd known what the real thing is like, I wouldn't ever—But I'm clean, Greg, I'm healthy. You don't need to worry about that."

I decided to try talking sense to Miss Sarah. "I think I'd like a word with my sister," I said, and he nodded his chin at me, appreciating my need, approving of it.

I left the groceries on the floor in the hall and ran up the stairs. Miss Sarah's room looked like the shirt scene in *Gatsby*, clothes all over the place. She had a small suitcase open on the bed. "I'd only have one suitcase, wouldn't I?"

"Miss Sarah—"

"I know what you're going to say and you can save your breath, Gregor. Can't you understand? If I had to, I'd trade the whole rest of my life just to have the night with him."

If she was going to be that way about it, there wasn't much I could do. I tried anyway. "Has it occurred to you, Miss Sarah, that you seem to rush around headlong?"

"I love him."

"Not enough to tell him the truth about who you are," I pointed out. But I didn't know why I should worry about it, worry over it.

"I will. I intend to. When it's the right time." As long as she got her way in the present moment, she was willing to promise to be reasonable at some future time.

"What about your parents?"

"I'm not a little girl. I can't spend my life pleasing my

parents, the way Prune has, and I don't want to. Look at what her life is like. You'll tell Theo for me, won't you?" She held up a nightgown, lace and silk. "Does this look too expensive? Just for my wedding night, it isn't, is it? Would a man notice?"

"I couldn't say, miss," I told her. After all, I thought, I might have better luck talking sense to Mr. Wycliffe. I went down the stairs, slowly.

"I can't help thinking you'd be wise to wait," I said to him. "Just another week or two, not long. I can't help thinking you don't know one another very well."

He laughed and clasped my shoulder in a fraternal gesture. "You don't expect me to give her up, do you? Relax, Greg. You see her like a brother. You probably can't imagine how I feel about her."

That at least was true. He was not, however, to be moved. I went back inside, back upstairs.

"What if I tell him the truth?"

That got her attention. "No, Gregor. Oh, please don't. Don't you have any sympathy for me? Haven't you ever been in love? It's not as if he's the wrong kind of man—He's someone they'd want me to marry, if they knew. Isn't he?"

"But not this way, miss. Suddenly. In secrecy like this. Leaving everybody else out of it."

"That's the way love has happened to us."

Love answered everything.

"Will you take my suitcase down?"

"If you were my sister—"

"But I'm not." She was tired of the game and eager to be on her way. "I'm your employer's sister. I'll deny it, Gregor, if you say anything. I'll deny it and he'll believe me."

I followed her down the stairs.

Outside, Mr. Wycliffe took the suitcase from me, as tenderly as if it were Sarah herself. "My car's around the corner, Sarah. Well, Greg, I look forward to knowing you better."

He meant it. He just didn't know what he meant. "Thank you, sir."

"Good-bye, Gregor," Miss Sarah said. "Wish me well?"

The girl should have gone into acting. "I wish you all happiness," I said, an appropriately ambiguous line. She stood up on tiptoe to kiss me on the cheek. It was prettily done.

I watched them walk away, arms around each other. They had already forgotten me. I couldn't imagine what Mr. Theo would say, when I had a chance to tell him the news.

"She *what*?" Mr. Theo demanded.

I had told him as plainly as possible. He had been sitting at his desk, looking at the mail.

"They *what*?" On the last word, he rose. His nostrils flared.

I passed him his scotch on the rocks. "Yes, sir."

"What is she thinking of? She never met him before, did she?"

"No."

"It's only been a week, then." He drank and sank back into his chair. "For God's sake. Why didn't you tell me she was seeing him?"

I didn't say anything.

"You should have stopped her."

"I did try, sir."

"Not very hard, apparently."

I left the room. Butler I was, cook, valet, housekeeper, occasional chauffeur—but not scapegoat. By the time Mr. Theo came out into the kitchen, I was making a salad, the greens spread out on the counter, crisp romaine, dark spinach, soft-leaved Boston. He brought me a glass of wine, a peace offering.

"I'm sorry, Gregor. She's my responsibility, not yours."

It was handsomely done, and I took the glass from him.

"The parents were wild enough that she'd left school. This will about finish them."

He watched me chiffonade the spinach. He lifted his glass and drank, with the muted sound of ice on heavy crystal.

" I don't know how Wycliffe could do this, after the crap he threw at me about his sister."

"He thought she was *my* sister," I told him.

"How could he think that?"

"It came about because of what you told her not to say, that first night."

"It just gets worse and worse," Mr. Theo said. "But what can I do?"

I couldn't advise him.

"Why did they elope? Why elope?"

"It's faster."

"What's their hurry?"

"Love, they said, sir."

"Love, my left foot. It's sex and they just don't know any better." He paced the kitchen. "Oh well, there is a bright side. It's not as if she's run off with some rock star or the chauffeur or some weedy Frenchman after her money. And do you know what I did today?"

I turned to look at him, to shake my head. He might as well have asked if I cared what he'd done. Looking proud and foolish, he pulled a small, square velvet box out of his pocket. He opened it and held it out for me to take. It *was* impressive, the diamond probably three or four carats, the emeralds that flanked it at least two each, I don't know very much about gemstones. It glittered and shone.

"I'm going to do it," Mr. Theo announced. "Propose. This weekend, if I get a chance." His face was resolute, Saul after Damascus. His voice was firm, ready to hear the doctor's diagnosis.

The phone rang then. Mr. Theo shook his head, directing me not to answer. He wanted me to continue admiring the ring. The answering machine cut in, and there was silence while the recorded message played. "I hope the young lady says yes, sir," I said.

"Why shouldn't she?" Mr. Theo asked, a rhetorical question.

The beep sounded, and the familiar throaty voice spoke. "Mr. Bear?" Mr. Theo looked at me. I was impassive. "It's been a few days, and last time you said call to remind you I was alive. I'm alive, Mr. Bear."

By that time he had the phone off the hook. "Hi, hello, I just got in. Yes, hello to you too. I've been meaning to call. What, tonight? I don't know if…But I do need to get out, I've been working too hard. Yeah, it would be fun. An hour and a half, is that too soon for you?" He laughed. "Hold that thought," he said. "Yeah, me too."

He hung up the phone and held out his hand. I returned the ring to him. "If I know Prune, she'll say yes. Her parents are all for it. So are mine." He put the ring back into his pocket. "Why else would she have put up with all this? So I'll marry her, live in Connecticut, settle down. It's time I settled down. How do you think you'll like living in the country, Gregor?"

"I won't know unless I try it, sir."

"Isn't that the way with everything," Mr. Theo said. For a second, I wondered if he meant the idea to be discussed; certainly it was an idea worth some discussion. "I'd better shower; dinner in half an hour?" he asked.

"Of course."

"And my little sister is getting married too, tomorrow. Wycliffe thinks he's marrying beneath him, doesn't he? I'd like to see his face when he finds out who she is."

He left the room laughing.

19

TO THE MARRIAGE
OF TRUE MINDS

"Don't interrupt me." Alexis snapped it out, impatient. Even while I watched for remorse to appear on her face and noted a distinct lack of it, she went on. "It has nothing to do with what's just. It has to do with what's effective."

"What is it you're saying, economics is the moral absolute?"

That stopped her. She put a bite of lobster salad into her mouth, and chewed, and thought.

I wondered if we were having a fight. If so, I wondered whether I could take that as a good sign.

"Why is it," she asked, "that we think morality is so simple? No," and she raised her hand to keep me from answering. "We do, we think it's simple, and we think that ours is the right one. It's an historic premise in this country. Is that because people don't want to think things out, they just want to feel in the right?"

She was asking me. I tried to think of the answer to her question. Later, I promised myself, I would think about what had happened to the compliant woman I had been lunching with, before I'd made an offhand remark about economic sanctions.

"Speaking for myself," I said carefully, "morality seems the essence of civilization. To act rightly is what makes civilized life possible. Or, at least, to intend to act rightly."

"This from a man who walked away from his home, what? how long ago?"

It was like a punch in the stomach. "Fifteen years."

"And have you been back?" I shook my head. "Told them where you are?" I shook my head.

She waited.

"You don't know—" I began, but she brushed my words aside before I'd given them utterance.

"And you sit there condemning me for being a moral relativist. Don't deny it, it's what you were thinking."

"Most relativists are easier to get along with than you are," I snapped back.

"You could only think that if you haven't ever thought about relativity. I mean really thought."

"All right." I took a breath and tried to steer the conversation back to a less lively topic. "If rather than withdrawing economic supports in order to use the power of money to control attitudes of another nation—and I do see your argument—if instead you invest more heavily so that you can have more influence, that may take longer but might work better, I'll grant you that. What's the difference though? Isn't it the ends justifying the means? Which is the essence of moral relativity?"

I don't know if women tend to move from the abstract to the personal as a general rule; in this instance Alexis did. "You're right, of course," she said. "So give me your justification for leaving home."

"That wasn't what I was talking about," I protested. I hadn't suspected her of arrogance. "There's a difference between personal and public morality, you know that. You can't just dismiss that."

"Yes, I can," she countered, and then she grinned at me. "I shouldn't, and I don't want to, but I can. I won't, but that doesn't mean I can't."

Utterly unselfconscious, entirely confident: this was not the woman I'd thought her. The fluffy hair, the pastel wardrobe—they were like those amusement park photographic setups where you step behind the cowboy, or astronaut, and put your face through. Half my mind was engaged in the parry and thrust of the conversation; the other half was wondering what it would be like to lie on a pillow beside her mind.

I wondered what she thought of Warhol. I wanted to talk to her about alternative energy and alternative schooling and alternative lifestyles. I thought she might well have made her way through Adam Smith and could make him comprehensible to me. How did she explain herself to herself? I wondered, curious.

"You're an unusual woman, aren't you?"

And she withdrew. Somehow. Like a day lily folding up at evening, becoming limp and pallid. Because of what I said, although not because of me. I could see it happening, in her face, in her groping at the side of her chair for the little purse she'd set down there.

"I have to go." Her purse perched on her lap.

"So we aren't going to spend the afternoon together?"

"I'm sorry."

I could have persuaded her, I think, and I thought that she might have wanted me to. But I suspected that I shouldn't, because of what she might think when she had time to think it over.

"I'm sorry too," I said. I paid, we rose, we went outside to find a taxi, I put her into it and held the door open. "Have dinner with me, a week from Sunday. I'll let you know where, but in the meantime, think about this. I'm hoping to marry you. I'm going to ask you about that."

"But Gregor—"

"You've got ten days to think it over," I said, and bent down to kiss her good-bye. When I lifted my mouth from hers, she was smiling.

"It's eleven days," she said.

20

MR. THEO'S TALE

I spent the next Sunday afternoon alone at the Whitney, treated myself to a solitary dinner and a showing of Fellini's *8 1/2*, and arrived home a little after ten. Mr. Theo was in the kitchen, with a glass of beer and the envelopes for his taxes, one thick, one thin. He always mailed his taxes at the last minute. "Let the money work for me as long as it can," was his argument. I had mailed mine that morning, on the same principal. Mr. Theo looked quite comfortable, his shirttail out, his feet shoeless.

"Welcome home, have a beer," he greeted me. "You look magnificent, Gregor. What do you and your friends do, Sunday in New York?"

I didn't answer. He didn't notice. I got myself a beer and a glass, took off my coat, drank.

He was looking at me as if he'd never seen me before.

"The next time you go shopping for ties," he said, "get two of anything that appeals to you, would you? You do have friends, don't you?" He answered his own question, "You must, you're a personable guy."

One, maybe, I might have answered, if I'd been going to answer. It was a good question, unsettling. I'd never expected Mr. Theo to unsettle me. "Miss Sarah called this morning," I told him.

I wasn't sure he was listening.

"They are safely married and safely back. I've noted the phone number and address."

He nodded, inattentive.

"She has asked that she be the one to tell your parents her news, on their return."

"They're going to have a hell of a homecoming. I hope they're rested up." He waited. "Next Friday, isn't it?" He waited.

"I believe so."

"Could you put out a major dinner, Gregor? Saturday?"

"How formal a meal are you thinking of? For how many?"

"Aren't you even going to ask me?" he demanded.

"Sir?"

"If I did it."

Did what? I wondered. Then I remembered. Before I could ask, he told me. "The answer is yes, I did. There's no need to drink standing up, Gregor. Have a seat."

"Thank you, sir." Now that I noticed, he did look pleased with himself.

"And the other answer is also yes. But it wasn't the way I imagined, not at all. I was losing at Scrabble—so what

131

else is new? Pruny was by the window. And I'd better get to work to stop calling her that, hadn't I? She'd seemed restless all evening, not the way she usually is, not lumpish. The curtains were open: you never have to draw curtains out in Connecticut, there's nobody near enough to see in. I don't know what she was looking at. The light was on her hair and it looked…clean, incredibly clean. I don't know why I noticed that. So I asked her."

"Ah," I said. He'd wanted to tell the story and I happened to be there; like the Ancient Mariner, he'd seized on me.

"I said," Mr. Theo said, "'We ought to get married.'" He paused. I didn't say anything. "She said," he said, "'I think we'd better.'" He paused again. "The truth is, I thought she'd be pleased. Hell, I thought she'd be knocked off her feet and all that. But not Prune, she didn't turn a hair, as if she wasn't even surprised; she didn't even turn around to look at me. But then, we've known each other forever…In any case, we're having dinner on Wednesday."

"Here?" I was rather curious to see this woman.

"No, of course not. A restaurant. I plan to marry the girl, not seduce her. Do you think it's funny she was so… cool?"

I had no way of knowing.

"It's not as if there's anyone else; her parents would have told my parents. But I don't know anything about her past, do I? Maybe there once was somebody? But I doubt it. I think there's just me. She never talks about herself. But I'm damned if I know why she said yes."

"I'm sure she had good reasons," I reassured him.

He nodded, having no doubts. "I think Europe for

the honeymoon; I feel like being traditional. After we tell the parents there'll be an announcement in the *Times*, a June wedding. I haven't even kissed her, Gregor. I've never touched her. It's so Victorian."

I didn't tell him that my guess is that the Victorians were just like the rest of us—only they didn't talk about it. "Does that concern you, sir?"

"Concern, as in make me nervous? If she's going to be frigid?" He shook his head. "Not a bit, in fact it's the biggest turn-on in years. I haven't felt...I was almost shaking, I kid you not, sitting behind the stupid Scrabble board, I thought I wouldn't be able to stand up. It's going to be hell waiting until June. I've shocked you, haven't I?"

"No. It's understandable. I can understand it."

He laughed out loud. "I like to think of you dandling my children on your dignified knees. I like the picture. You will stay on, won't you?" He gave me no time to answer. "Connecticut is a good place to raise kids. You ought to get married yourself, Gregor."

I permitted myself: "I have been giving it some thought, sir."

"You have?" He lifted his glass to toast me. "You are? It must be something in the air. We're falling like flies."

21

WHAT THE MACHINE SAID

Word spread quickly. Isn't it Virgil who employs that metaphor about rumor's dark-winged flight? Only this, of course, was not rumor but truth. I wondered, bringing in the mail, turning on the machine to hear the morning's messages, if it could be said that truth flies as quickly as rumor. Socrates would dispute that. However, if I named it not truth but fact—except that the air is so full of flying facts, like bats in a boathouse, that all one can do is swing at them with a tennis racquet, bringing down as many as one can. Of Mr. Theo's engagement, however, it could be said that word spread quickly. An event of some note, it seemed.

Whirr, beep. "Teddy, it's Lisette. Congratulations, I think. I sure congratulate *her*. The truth is, if I'd known you were on the verge of marriage, I'd have handled you a little differently. And if that pleases your vanity, it's meant to. Best wishes to you, Teddy, best of luck. Sorry about… it all." *Beep.*

Whirr, beep. "Theo, Dad here. We've changed to a Thursday evening flight, so we can be rested up to join you Saturday. I'm sure you know how pleased we are." *Beep.*

Whirr, beep. "Well, I am impressed, little brother. It's Babbsy, remember me? Mother called last night and I'd hoped to catch you this morning before you went to work, but I guess—it's seven twenty-five, our time—But I'm impressed, the way they cut their stay short to come home and celebrate. Remember how much trouble we had fitting my wedding in between a trip to London and the Member-Guest Tournament? Comes from being a boy, you think? Or marrying the right person. Although I can't imagine why Prune is marrying you, unless she figures she knows you at your worst so there's nothing horrible to discover. I guess you know what you're doing, you two. I should say congratulations. I guess I do. Sorry to be cynical, and I do hope everything goes well for you. You're older than I was; maybe you'll be smarter. I don't get too excited anymore about weddings, mine or anyone else's, but I'll be there, with bells on, you can bet on that. If you're happy, I'm happy for you." *Beep.*

Whirr, beep. "Ted. Kyle. What do you want to go and do a thing like that for? Just kidding, buddy. Seriously. I lay claim to hosting your bachelor party, so give me a date. We're falling like flies, have you noticed?" *Beep, whirr.*

Beep. "It's Christine Rawling, Theo, to say first that we are all glad to accept your invitation to dinner Saturday, and second how pleased Martin and I are at your news.

We think you'll be very happy with our girl. We'll tell you so in person on Saturday. That's at seven thirty, isn't it?" *Beep, whirr.*

Beep. "Theo, Davy here. Well done, little brother, the parents are all in a dither and Alice and the kids are pretty excited too. I'll be proud to be your best man—returning the favor. Call me tonight. I'll be in meetings most of the day, then coaching, so it better be after dinner. You won't regret it, Theo, that's my brotherly advice." *Beep.*

Whirr, beep. "This is Reverend Smallquist's office returning Mr. Mondleigh's call. If Mr. Mondleigh could get back to us as soon as possible, with the date he wants, the Reverend is holding all open spaces in his calendar until he hears from Mr. Mondleigh." *Beep, beep, beep.*

22

CARELESS LOVE

I reserved a table at Le Cirque, and a small suite upstairs at the Mayfair as well. I couldn't be sure how Alexis would answer me, but it seemed wise to have a place ready, should bedding her be part of the evening. I had always avoided trading in futures, but this once it seemed reasonable.

By the middle of the week leading up to the Sunday that would tell my fate, I had everything ready. It remained only to await the event, and to prepare Mr. Theo's engagement dinner.

In fact, I fully expected Alexis to turn me down. There are, however, many ways of declining, and many of those are postponements. She would decline, I would persist, and, with luck, eventually…

I opened the door on Wednesday morning to bring in the mail but found instead Miss Sarah, seated on the

137

stoop, her dark head bent into her hands, her suitcase on the sidewalk. She looked up at me and her face was wet, as if she had just come in from the rain, although the sun shone on her. I looked more carefully. She was weeping. "Miss Sarah. Let me bring your suitcase in," I said. "Excuse me, Mrs. Wycliffe."

She preceded me into the house. "The suitcase goes upstairs, Gregor. To my room. And it's Miss Sarah."

I had to make up the bed, open the windows to freshen the air, and be sure the bathroom was properly supplied. By the time I got back downstairs, she was in the kitchen. The kettle was on the stove and she had a teapot out and a cup. "I'm looking for honey."

"I'll do that, miss," I offered. "Would you like something to eat with your tea?"

She fidgeted with the teapot, with the cup and saucer, with the spoon. She wore a short black skirt and a black long-sleeved leotard. She wore a gold band on her left hand. "I'm not hungry."

She took the top off the kettle. Looked in. Replaced the top. She moved the teapot around on the counter. And sighed. And squared her shoulders. And turned around to tell me. "I've left him."

"Oh?" It didn't seem kind to say that I'd guessed as much.

"I packed up everything that's mine, and he'll never have to know I was ever there." She was resolute and brave.

"Ah," I said.

"I thought"—her voice quivered, and she controlled it—"he loved me."

"Ah," I said, and the kettle whistled. She looked helplessly at it. I guided her to a chair and prepared the tea. She was weeping again, so I tactfully ignored her, except to put the box of tissues near to hand.

By the time the tea had steeped and her cup was poured, she had blown her nose and was ready to explain.

"He said, he thought I was good and pure and beautiful, but now he knows I'm a liar and a cheat. When I told him. Who I was. This morning, because I didn't want to lie to him. I didn't want to live a lie. He hadn't even looked at the marriage license. He could have looked at it if he wanted to know, after I signed it. He asked me if I was really a dancer and I had to tell the truth. I couldn't lie to him. So he walked out."

"This morning?"

She nodded.

"Wasn't he going to work?"

"Just walked out, without saying anything, and he didn't come back and he hasn't called. He said I never loved him because you don't lie to someone you love. What does a lie matter, if you love someone? Love matters, that's what matters."

I went to the phone and pushed the button that would connect me to Mr. Theo's office.

"I tried to tell him," and tears were once again running down her cheeks. "I tried, but he wouldn't believe me. If I didn't love him, I wouldn't care enough to lie to him. He said that was just the kind of argument he'd expect me to use." She pulled out tissues.

"I wonder if you might come home, sir," I asked. "Miss Sarah is here, in some distress."

"He's spoiled everything," Miss Sarah wailed.

Mr. Theo apparently heard that. "I'm on my way."

"We were like Romeo and Juliet," she cried, "but he never loved me."

"Your brother is on his way, miss," I promised her.

That stopped her tears. "Theo's why Brad hates me. I don't want to see Theo. I don't want him to come here."

"This *is* his house," I reminded her gently. "He *is* your brother."

"But he doesn't understand. Nobody understands." She lifted her face. "I could learn how to dance. I could become a dancer."

"If I may say something?" I asked her.

"As long as you don't tell me you told me so."

"Romeo and Juliet," I told her, "did not live happily ever after."

It was the wrong thing, absolutely wrong. Her expression crumpled into misery, her face fell forward onto the table, and she sobbed.

Miss Sarah moped and wept for most of that day and the next, until eventually she arrived at sorrow, with an occasional backsliding into misery. I put her to work and by Saturday morning we were an efficient couple, I forming *pâte à choux* for profiteroles, she chopping onions and carrots and celery for the base on which I would roast veal.

I did feel sorry for her. She was so young, and the young man was little older. I could see why certain societies married young women to older, more patient men; even though it established patterns for which all women were still paying the price, there was something to be said for it. Unless the society could learn to do better by its young men, unless society could come to see how little it makes of its men. Women, at least, are trying to look out for themselves.

"You mustn't cry like that, Miss Sarah," I said.

"How am I supposed to cry?"

"Your mother will be sure to think there's something wrong."

"There is something wrong. Everything's wrong."

"Yes, miss," I said. "But if you don't want your parents to know, if you don't want everyone to know, you're going to have to do a better job of pretending."

"I know." She took another carrot to hack at and hacked energetically. "I will try. Mornings are the worst, because it's so…sad. I'm twenty and I've been happy for three weeks, and now it's over. That's sad, isn't it? I'm never going to be happy again." She scraped carrot chunks into a waiting bowl and took up celery. "I wish I'd never met him, I really do. He said he never wanted to see me again. How could he say that?"

Mr. Theo entered on the question. "How could who say what?" One look at his sister answered him. "Oh. Brad again. Never mind, Sarah, you'll forget him."

"Never."

"I don't know what you saw in him anyway. He's a stick and a prude and not nearly good enough for you. Is everything set for tonight, Gregor?" Mr. Theo was dressed for a game of tennis. He picked up a celery stalk and munched on it.

"At least Brad's not a—a womanizer. You wouldn't

find Brad getting phone calls from women who won't leave their names."

Mr. Theo turned her around by the shoulders. "What phone calls?"

"While you were out with your fiancée." Miss Sarah purred, a kitten imitating a cat, "The Voice."

"Why didn't you tell me?"

"I just did. Mr. Bear." Anger at least distracted her from her own sorrows. "It's sickening, Theo. I have half a mind to tell."

"Don't even think of it, Sarah."

"Anyway, I don't think The Voice believed that I'm your sister."

"And I bet you did everything you could to convince her."

"Well honestly, Theo," Miss Sarah pointed out, "she sounds…You know what she sounds like."

I put the laden tray into the oven and set the timer.

"At least she's no hypocrite," he said.

It was a genuine brother-sister spat, the kind of fight you could only have with a brother or sister, saying the kinds of things you would only say to a brother or sister. If you said them to anyone else, it would be the end of the relationship. For the first time in fifteen years, I found myself thinking longingly of family life.

"And just what do you mean by that?" Miss Sarah demanded.

"You know what I mean. You know exactly what I mean. I mean calling a spade a spade. I mean calling it lust, Sarah. Not dressing it up and calling it love, marriage. Then sighing and weeping and doing this great tragedy act when it goes bad. You can mess up your own life, but don't go messing around in mine." He strode out of the room. We heard the front door slam.

"But he isn't being fair to her, is he, Gregor?"

I didn't see that it mattered but didn't say so.

"I don't know why she's marrying him anyway. She's awfully nice, and Theo's—he can be a bully."

"Perhaps she loves him," I suggested.

"I don't think so. I think it's more a matter of getting so old that it's now or never for her. He won't be faithful."

"Perhaps that isn't what matters to her," I said. "Besides, maybe he will."

"I'd die if I thought Brad—" She gulped, and started again. "But that's what men do, isn't it. Instead of crying all morning, they sleep around. He hasn't called, and he could figure out where I am. So he doesn't love me. Theo's right. He never did."

She was reducing herself to tears again. I'd never been an older brother before, but I thought that since she needed one, I ought to attempt it.

"Try to see it as he must, Miss Sarah. Imagine how humiliating it would be if you came to the rescue and rode off with the little goose girl—only to discover that she had never needed your help at all, and wasn't even a goose girl. Some people don't like being laughed at, miss."

"But I didn't laugh," she protested. "What am I going to do, Gregor?"

"First, finish the vegetables, so I can start them browning. Then, spend the afternoon getting pretty, for dinner. It's a dinner with your brother's fiancée and her parents, and your parents, where you're going to be young and care-free, and nobody will suspect how you really feel."

"I think I'll wear black."

"Wear yellow," I advised, "or something flowery, floating, or a bright blue. Remember, it's a masquerade. The masquerade is that you are young and irresponsible and silly."

I'd captured her imagination. "I'll try. I don't think I can do that though."

23

GOD AS A HUMORIST

Of course I know that if there is a God—or a life force, or fate, or any governing power else that human creatures perceive in hope or hope to perceive—he or she is not concerned with my personal history. But sometimes, when the ironies pile up, it seems as if he, or she, or it, must be meddling. Oedipus gouges out his eyes; Cleopatra takes an asp to her breast: *I should have known*, I said to myself. *You should have known.*

There I was, my mind and spirit bent to the next evening's possibilities, barely attending to the presentation of Mr. Theo's dinner. There they were, the hosts awaiting, the dinner guests arriving. There we all were.

Miss Sarah, slim as a dancer in a red dress, watched at the window. "They're here, Theo." Darkly sartorial, he left to greet them by an open door. I set down linen cocktail napkins and the ice bucket. "If they use a limo in the city, it's them. Yes," Miss Sarah said, "with Allie in the middle like a sacrificial lamb. And Mummy's with them, and Dad." She went to stand beside her brother. "They're so tan."

Returning to the kitchen to prepare the soup bowls, I was overtaken by a forceful female voice. "My daughter says she's never seen your house, Theo. I approve of that. There's entirely too much of this seeing one another's houses before marriage. Marriage should hold some surprises."

It was the voice of a woman for whom marriage, and life, held few surprises, and that was the way she liked it. I felt a qualm of sympathy for Mr. Theo.

Also, I admit it, a frisson of *It serves him right.* I was smirking over the madrilene, which I dished into chilled bowls, topped with a sprinkling of herbs and a lemon slice, then carried out to the table. The dinner party was disporting itself in the living room, not my responsibility; I poured iced water into goblets, after which I refilled the silver pitcher with ice and water and set it on the sideboard. A final glance around, to assure myself that everything was as it should be—the floral arrangements low enough so that they didn't interfere with seated conversation, the bottles of wine ready, three rosettes of butter on each butter plate— and I went out into the living room, to announce dinner.

Entering the living room, plumped out with the success of both of my roles…It was the ring I saw first, emeralds flanking the marquise diamond, heavy on the little hand, and by the time I realized I recognized the hand, and the woman, I had already announced dinner. I didn't look at her, I didn't have to. I felt the shock with which she heard my voice. It seemed to me that the air between us congealed. It seemed to me that her head must have snapped up, snapped around.

Some men might have gotten angry, some might have wept, some might have gouged out their eyes, and some—like me—would have stood in the kitchen, *rictus sardonicus. You should have known,* I said to myself. Then I canceled thought.

When the buzzer summoned me, I entered the dining room to clear the soup bowls. Seven people were ranged about the table: Alexis sat at the far end, opposite Mr. Theo, the two men sat side by side so that Mr. Mondleigh could sit at Alexis's right, and the three women sat across from them, so that Mrs. Rawling could sit at Mr. Theo's right. Miss Sarah was tucked into the middle, like a child. I latched the swinging door open, to move more unnoticeably. Conversation went on; my presence made no difference to the assembly.

At formal meals I carried platters and bowls of food around, bending down confidentially at the left shoulder to enable each guest to serve himself. Or herself. Host and guests talked on, as I cleared the soup course, brought warmed plates out and set one at each place, offered food around, and then poured wine into each glass. On such occasions, I was a long time in the dining room.

"It took them a while, Martin," Mr. Mondleigh remarked, "but they did us right, in the end."

"Congratulations, you two," Mr. Rawling seconded, looking from one end of the table to the other. The two fathers, side by side, could have been clones of one another, for all the surface differences. Two well-satisfied men.

"We wish you all the best." Mr. Mondleigh raised

his glass, first to his son, then to his son's fiancée. "Don't we, Elaine?"

"Yes, of course." Mrs. Mondleigh raised her own glass obediently. "Although…"

Mrs. Rawling leapt into the caesura. "Not too quickly with some of that, such as children." She had her daughter's direct mind, as well as nose and deep eyes. Both she and her husband had unusually unlined faces; Alexis would wear well, I thought. She would probably keep, as her parents had, that wonderful porcelain skin well into her later years.

Mr. Rawling cleared his throat, importantly. "Allie will maintain her holdings in her own name, of course. You might not guess it, Theo, but my little girl has a good business head on those pretty shoulders."

The pretty shoulders were not visible, underneath a white dress bordered at the high collar and long sleeves with pink and blue embroidered flowers, as if she were some eighteen-year-old debutante. With her head lowered, her hair covered her cheeks as I put a dinner plate in front of her. I was pretty sure she didn't look at me to see that I wasn't looking at her. Her hands rested in her lap, still.

"Of course, Martin, I wouldn't have it any other way. My firm will draw up the nuptial agreement. Not that we expect these two to need it."

"What about our wills?" Mr. Theo asked. His voice sounded sincere but his nostrils were flaring slightly. "You haven't forgotten about wills, have you, Dad?"

"Don't tease your father, Theo," Mrs. Mondleigh counseled.

Mrs. Rawling dismissed all this. "Tonight, of all nights, is not the time to discuss property. You two can settle that on your next round of golf." She helped herself to a serving of veal, spooning sauce over it generously. "Allie isn't thinking about that at all, are you dear? Of course you aren't."

I didn't dare to think what Alexis might be thinking.

"Allie has a wedding to think about," Mrs. Rawling announced.

I set the meat platter on a sideboard and went into the kitchen for a bowl of rice, which I bore out into the dining room.

Mrs. Rawling still held the floor. "Only half a dozen attendants apiece, maybe ten, a smallish wedding, as intimate as possible. Ask Sarah," she instructed her daughter.

"I hope you'll be a bridesmaid, Sarah," Alexis asked.

"Sure," Miss Sarah said. "Thanks. I'd love to."

Mr. Theo was gazing off over his fiancée's head, his thoughts elsewhere.

"Yellow for the church," Mrs. Rawling went on, "we thought, with lime green for emphasis color. Then we'll do the clubhouse in lime green, with yellow for emphasis. A daffodil yellow, rather pale."

Nobody had anything to say. I offered rice. Nobody could find anything to say, so Miss Sarah offered, "That sounds nice."

"There should be no trouble putting up the out-of-town guests. We both have room, and there's also your parents' house, David—it's empty, isn't it?—where we thought the ushers might stay, and their families, if any are married. Are any of your ushers married, Theo? Will there be any children?"

Mr. Theo brought himself back to attention. Before

he could answer, his father did. "The old house won't be available."

"Oh?" queried Mrs. Rawling. She was a little offended, or rather, she was prepared to be a little offended.

"Oh, hell. I wasn't going to tell you yet, Theo, but I guess this is as good a time as any. We're giving you your grandfather's house as a wedding present."

"That's handsome," Mr. Rawling said, "I must say." The two men faced each other, satisfaction washing between them like water trapped in a tub. I offered asparagus.

"What do you think of that, Allie?" her mother demanded. "What do you say?"

"We're giving Allie title to the house on Lake George," Mr. Rawling announced.

Mr. Theo wanted to laugh. This gave his voice a choked quality, as if he were deeply moved. "That's very generous, Mr. Rawling."

"Call me Martin, son."

"Have some asparagus, Miss Sarah," I murmured. Her hands clutched at her napkin, and her mouth pulled down at the edges. I thought I knew how she felt, just about.

"You'll want a place to get away to. To be by your-selves," Mrs. Rawling explained.

Miss Sarah smiled bravely at me.

"Allie's always loved the lake," Mr. Rawling explained. "From when she was just a little girl. Haven't you, sweetheart?"

"Yes," Alexis said.

"It's awfully…" Mrs. Mondleigh began.

"Generous," Mrs. Rawling finished the thought. "Considering the price of land on Lake George. But she's our only child, after all. When you've only the one child, you want to give her everything."

"Nothing's too much for our Allie," Mr. Rawling echoed.

"But"—Mrs. Rawling cut short the display of parental fondness—"there's so much to decide, and they're only giving me six weeks. You'll be doing the same yourself, before long, Sarah. This will be good practice for you."

I offered the plate of asparagus to Mr. Theo.

"I'm surprised you didn't worry, Elaine, with Sarah at school abroad," Mrs. Rawling said.

"Worry about what?"

"So far away, and out of touch, didn't you worry that she'd meet someone?"

"That was the point," Mr. Theo said. "Wasn't it, Dad? To broaden her horizons."

"What if she'd wished to marry over there?" Mrs. Rawling asked.

Mr. Mondleigh answered. "With Sarah we're more afraid she'll never settle down at all."

"Oh, I wouldn't worry about that, David," Mr. Rawling assured him. "Sarah will catch someone's eye, no fear for that. You'll meet the right man. Girls do," he promised her. "Especially pretty girls."

"But how could my parents be sure he wouldn't be Swiss, this right man?" Miss Sarah asked. "Or Hungarian?"

"You're making fun of us," Mrs. Mondleigh observed.

"He could have been, of course," Mrs. Rawling said. "It's possible, of course. Just not likely. Luckily for my peace of mind, Allie has never had much desire to travel."

"Oh no!" Mr. Theo clapped his hand against his

forehead. I filled the glasses with wine. "What about the honeymoon?"

Mrs. Rawling was not to be put off. "You know what I meant, not travel for travel's sake."

"Is that true, Allie?" Mrs. Mondleigh asked. "I thought every young person wanted to…"

I returned the wine bottle to the sideboard.

"See the world," Mr. Mondleigh finished the thought for his wife. I took a last look around the table.

"Not Allie," Mr. Rawling said. "Not our Allie. Isn't that right, sweetheart?"

They lifted their forks, to begin the meal.

"I think it must be," Alexis said.

I left, unhooking the swinging door so that it could close behind me. In the living room I put the bar table away and cleared the glasses. I rinsed those glasses and the soup bowls and loaded them into the dishwasher. I started scouring pans.

There must be a moment when you see that your plane has been hit. You've been dodging about through enemy fire and the engine bursts into flame, or a wing falls off. There must be a moment of perception—I am about to go down, I've had it, that's it for me, I'm sunk, *tutto è finito*—a moment as you spiral down to meet the ground that rises, rushing, at you. Then after the perception but preceding the event, a moment for understanding. Knowledge. That whole evening seemed to me such a moment, dragging out interminably. I only awaited the ground.

The buzzer summoned me, and I dried my hands, took off my apron, latched the swinging door. I cleared the dinner dishes and brought in the dessert—each plate holding three little puff pastries, each pastry filled with *crème pâtissière* and napped with a thin sauce of bitter chocolate.

"I'd like to be based out at the Farm," Mr. Theo was saying. "I haven't made up my mind what to do with this house. I haven't held it long enough to make much of a profit on the investment."

"Rent it to me," Miss Sarah offered. "I'll rent it, if you'll leave me Gregor."

He ignored her. "Some days I'll probably have to stay in town. I put in some long hours some days, and there are business dinners."

"I keep hearing your name, Theo," Mr. Rawling said. "You're building yourself something of a reputation."

Mr. Mondleigh was pleased. "Theo doesn't just sit back and let the world carry him. Neither of my sons does."

"And your daughters?" Miss Sarah asked.

Ripe with wine and well-being, he took no offense. "You're thinking of Babbsy," he deduced. "Your sister's not a good example of anything, but women, girls, daughters— their role in society is different from men's role. To have children. Be protected. Babbsy simply has no judgment about her men."

"Women make a home," Mr. Rawling added. "Preserve culture, you know, the arts. You haven't been turned into a radical over there, have you, Sarah? You're entirely too pretty for that."

Sarah bridled, and Alexis looked uncomfortable, and even Mrs. Mondleigh was gazing thoughtfully at the men.

"Sarah?" her father asked. "You aren't thinking of going to work, are you? What qualifications do you have? You don't have any qualifications, do you?"

Mrs. Rawling answered for her. "We'll need Sarah full-time, until we get this wedding off our hands. Your mother will need your help, Sarah, and somebody will have to oversee the redecoration of the old house."

"Doesn't Allie want to do that?" Sarah asked.

"I'll need Allie to help me. You have no idea, either of you girls, what a job it is to put on a wedding. And at such short notice. Allie and I will have our hands full, and I'm sure you have lovely taste. You two"—she switched her attention—"will have to decide immediately on silver and china, glassware. I should know those by the first of the week, so Allie can be registered."

I unlatched the door and let it swing closed behind me. There was the coffee tray to set up and take out to the living room; there were more pots to be scrubbed clean and the dinner dishes. If I felt hungry later, I'd eat then.

The sound of muffled conversation faded when the party rose from the table. The kitchen door swung open and I turned off the running water, wiped my hands on my apron.

Mrs. Rawling was speaking to Alexis as they entered. "You begin as you mean to go on," she advised. "Ah—?" She'd forgotten my name. "My daughter would like a word."

"Gregor," Alexis supplied. Her eyes were like a firing squad.

"That's right, Gregor." Mrs. Rawling left us together.

Alexis stood where she had been set, like a dumpling dropped on the kitchen floor. I gave her a few seconds, then carried a handful of silverware to put it into the dishwasher. She would cry shame, I knew, and maybe shed a tear for her deceived self. I wasn't going to help her. "Yes, miss?"

"It was an excellent dinner," Alexis said.

So I had never happened. "Thank you, miss." I could pretend as well as the next man. Or woman.

She seemed to have nothing more to say, so I went back to work.

"Theo says," she began, and I turned off the water, turned around again. "Theo says you are a treasure."

"He exaggerates, miss," I said. This time I stood and waited, until she had finished whatever piece she planned to speak. I owed her the chance; I knew that.

"Will you be staying on with Theo? After?" she asked.

"Are you giving me my notice?"

"I can't do that, you work for Theo. You know that, Gregor." I had made her impatient. "But—" And she looked at me, really looked at me. "What were you thinking of? How could you do that to me?" There was no self-pity in her voice, only curiosity and an angry protest.

"I didn't know who you were, miss."

"You didn't know exactly, but you knew."

She was right. I couldn't deny it.

"I don't see how you *could* stay on. With us. After. And it makes me angry, Gregor. I guess I really will marry Theo now. I guess I have to. I guess I'd really better." She laughed. "I thought—it's incredible—I thought I could always run away to my mysterious admirer, if my parents were wrong about Theo asking me, if it wasn't going to work out. I thought, it wasn't as if there was only Theo to marry. And I didn't know that was what I was thinking. That's frightening, isn't it? Did you know I was thinking that?"

"Not precisely that," I told her.

"I was thinking I had a choice, but—What a rotten

thing to do to Theo, Gregor. How could you do that to him?"

That, at least, I hadn't done, at least not intentionally.

"I guess I gave you a lot of help, didn't I? Oh, I am such a fool. I should have known, or suspected at least. And I did, sort of—but not this. But I don't understand how you could do it. No, never mind. I know, I do know, and I even understand why. I think I must have known all along, or at least suspected. I'm sorry. I don't blame you, not really. I blame myself. I was using you just about the same way you were using me, wasn't I."

It was not a question. It was just the truth. She waited, then, for whatever I might want to say.

"You're not a fool, Alexis," I promised her.

She thought that over, watching my face. "Yes I am," she finally said. "I shouldn't be let out without a keeper. I'm lucky Theo thinks it would be smart to marry me, or otherwise—"

She didn't need to finish that sentence.

24

LIFE GOES ON

The *Times* printed the announcement without delay, so that—as Mrs. Rawling put it—nobody should think there was a question of necessity. No necessary marriage this. "A June wedding is planned," the announcement read. Mr. Theo had already sent invitations out to his friends, asking them to come celebrate the occasion with him, over a few drinks.

While I waited for Miss Sarah to finish packing, I listened to the answering machine, guest list in hand, to record acceptances. *Whirr, beep*.

Beep. "Teddy? Muffy, and I'd love to come, I accept with pleasure, I'm so happy for you both. Can I bring a friend? I'll assume so, unless you tell me not to; I sort of figured with cocktails numbers don't really matter. I look forward to it. Allie sure lucked out." *Beep*.

I checked off the name, and noted *plus one* beside it.

Whirr, beep. "Lisette here, Teddy. I wasn't going to accept, but I am, but I'm bringing a friend, and I do want to lay eyes on this lady." *Beep.* I checked the name, noted *plus one.*

Whirr, beep. "Theo, it's Mother. Sarah seems to want to stay on in the city, with you, for a few days she said. I've given her permission. I'm a little...uneasy about her, Theo. She seems to be...making herself ill about something. Can you cast any light? Is there a man? Is that why she left school?" *Beep, whirr.*

Beep. "Pete here, Ted. Sure, I'll be there. Alone, though—Sal and I broke up. Hope you don't mind. God knows I don't."

I checked off the one name and crossed out the other. *Beep, whirr.*

Beep. "I read the papers, Mr. Bear, and I hope you'll be happy. I sincerely mean that. I do. Remember, I never said I had anything against married men. Or engaged men." *Beep.*

My sympathy for Alexis was short-lived, and insincere.

Whirr, beep. "Teddy? It's Wendy and I've got a sitter, so Stu and I will be there, with bells on. To welcome you to the fold." *Beep.*

I heard footsteps descending the stairs and fast-forwarded the machine to the end of the recordings, then reset it. I left the invitation list beside it, so that I could pick up where I'd left off. I put on my peaked chauffeur's hat.

Miss Sarah waited by the stairs. An overnight case was at her feet. She looked resolute and unhappy. I opened my mouth.

"I know what you're going to say, Gregor, and you

needn't bother. I got myself into this and in a couple of days I'll be back, and I'll have gotten myself out. Mexican divorces are legal enough."

She wore a simple black suit and a soft white blouse. A black purse hung from her shoulder. She could have been going out to see her lawyer or investment counselor, or to buy a serious antique.

"Do you have money?" I asked her.

"Traveler's cheques, tickets, hotel reservation."

"Something to read?" I asked.

At that she smiled. "Something to—? What would I read?"

I took the thick paperback copy of *War and Peace* out of my jacket pocket. "Forty-eight hours can be a long time. If you're alone, and waiting."

She wrapped her fingers around it. "Thanks. Thank you. I *do* like you, Gregor. You were right, even though you never said so. I should have told him the truth."

I picked up the little case. "I don't know, miss, the truth is no guarantee of anything. But if we're going to make a two-thirty flight…The car is right out front."

She nodded. I followed her out the door.

25

RITES OF PASSAGE

From my place behind the bar in the living room, I could oversee the workings of the party. Waitresses moved about, offering trays of artfully wrought, colorfully assorted canapés. Mr. Theo moved among his guests. Alexis, I assumed, was doing the same in the library, accepting congratulations. The long living room, at one end of which I stood, was noisy with conversation, the air thick with perfumes and colognes, the space crowded with bodies, limbs, faces. I overheard scraps of conversations, as glasses were asked of me or handed to me to refill, and I poured wines, whiskeys, gin, vodka, adding cubes of ice or twists of lemon where appropriate.

• • •

"The scenery in the Alps I give you, but the trails are like everything else in Europe, graded to a different degree of difficulty than I'm used to. It's like buying clothes in France, I'm always ready to discover I've read the trail wrong and ski into an abyss, or an avalanche. Give me Sun Valley any day. There I'm—"

"Losing Teddy to such a dumpy—I know it's not kind, but honestly, she is. I don't see what he sees in her. It's not as if he was looking for intellectual companionship—"

"I run three miles a day, at least, gave up smoking, only drink wine, and I'm so much sharper—"

"I very much doubt she'll go on for the degree now. What does someone need with a second doctorate who never really needed the first?"

"Still, it was good of her to invite us. And she is bright enough, a good student."

"Yes, very sound. Often thoughtful. Too much money, of course."

• • •

"The earrings? Phil gave them to me, just before I left him. As if you can *buy* love."

"It can't be love, do you think? Not money either. I think, it just gets to be time, and people think they ought to get married. Teddy's the right age for it, isn't he? Early thirties?"

"Not to mention that her biological clock is ticking. It's safer too. I don't blame them. Does she garden, like her parents?"

"She goes to school, that's all I know. But it's not as if Teddy is any more interested in education than gardens. Although I do think they're doing the right thing."

"—trapped in this endless round of his business engagements. We don't have any friends, I certainly don't, we just see a lot of people who might be useful to us. They're just useful people we see. Just people we see."

"Two years at the outside, that's what I give it. He'll be bored long before that, and as soon as he's bored, he'll be available again. No, I'm not upset."

• • •

"—sixty-feet, gaff-rigged, you'll have to come out on her someday, it was a lucky buy. One of those oilmen whose fortune disappeared on him. I paid half what it cost him."

"She's lucky to catch him, that's all I can say. She's had a crush on him for years."

"Has she? I wonder why."

"You've got to be kidding."

"They don't have anything in common. Except background, upbringing. But have you ever tried to talk to Teddy? I mean, exchange ideas? It's like trying to talk to my father. I'd go crazy."

"But you're not Allie."

"No, and she seems happy enough."

"Never mind them, what about us? I told you from the start it was marriage I wanted, and it seems to me that everybody I know is getting married. Except me. Always excepting me. I'm beginning to think there's something wrong with me. Or with you, Bobby."

Briefer than a rose, the party bloomed and faded. Mr. Theo and Alexis stood side by side as they sped the departing guests. Her hair had gone limp, as had his smile. As I closed the door behind the last couple, she said, "I'm too tired for dinner, Theo. I'm sorry, but—"

"Hey, that's OK. Maybe I'll drag Sarah out of her room, take her out to cheer her up, or something. Gregor will drive you home: I'm too lit to be behind the wheel of a car. Hell, I'm not all that hungry myself. Is ten tomorrow morning going to be too early for you?"

"No."

"It might be for me, so I guess you can expect me when you see me. We'll have the whole afternoon for looking the house over, which is more time than I'll need."

I went to get my coat and cap. The waitresses were finishing up in the kitchen. Mr. Theo walked her to the car, and I drove her to 1195 Park. There, I went around to open the door and hand her out. "Thank you, Gregor," she said, and didn't look at me.

"Good night, miss," I said. I didn't blame her.

Frankly, it was a pretty dismal time for me. I'd had other opportunities, a few, but none of them so protracted, none so promising as Alexis. The pattern had been a couple of meetings, a room at the Pierre or the Plaza, a few days, maybe a week, and then she'd tell me she was leaving town—for the West Coast, for abroad, for anywhere else— and didn't know when she'd be back. I knew I had had my own purpose for those women, and they had had their own uses for me. The experiences had been frustrating, no more. I had felt the way Gauguin must have felt, looking at his paintings, before he went to Tahiti. Alexis had looked like Tahiti.

And now she was sitting in the back of the Mercedes, which I drove, beside her fiancé, for whom I worked. All had been revealed. All was lost. It was entirely dismal and I found myself curiously debilitated by the experience.

We left the city and arrived at the Connecticut Turnpike; we looped along the shore at sixty-five miles an hour. I don't know if they talked; the window was raised. I don't know if they necked or held hands; I didn't look into the rearview mirror. We left the turnpike and went inland for a few miles, until the gate of the Farm appeared on my right. I turned into the estate, but instead of bearing right, to approach the Mondleigh home, I kept on straight, to the old house, the original house, set on the highest point of the property with a view of the distant Sound.

Impassive, I held the car doors for them. Mr. Theo seemed ill at ease when he stood on the Belgian brick driveway and looked up at the pale stucco facade. "Gregor, you'd better come in with us. This has as much to do with you as anyone else," he said.

"Yes, sir."

We walked through long, high-ceilinged rooms, where furniture sat shrouded in dusty air. We walked around the large kitchen, then back through the butler's pantry to the breakfast room and into the dining room. We ascended the main staircase. They were silent. I followed them. By the time we arrived at the master bedroom, Mr. Theo was both bored and uneasy. I stood in the doorway. They entered. Each arrived at the foot of one of the two massive beds. Both looked around the room without looking at one another.

"You'll probably want a decorator in," Mr. Theo said.

"Yes." She made an effort. "Are there colors you prefer, Theo?"

"No, it doesn't matter, I never thought about it. Look, Allie, I need to see Dad about some business. Anything you decide is all right with me. Anyway, Gregor has better taste than I do. You two will probably work better without me. Don't bother, Gregor, I'll walk. It's not far. I could use the fresh air."

I stepped back to let him pass by me. I returned to the doorway, hat in hand. Alexis turned around, looked at me, turned away…embarrassed, was my guess.

"If you'll excuse me, miss?" I asked her.

"Yes, thank you." She sat down on the edge of the bed and studied the carpet.

I went back down to the kitchen, then ascended a narrow back staircase to the servants' wing. Three bedrooms, one with its own sitting room and a private bath, a low sloping ceiling and flowered wallpaper. A double bed, iron, painted white, occupied this bedroom. I sat down on it, hat in hand. The ceiling seemed to press down on me.

I thought about what I would want to do with the room and its sitting room, with the servants' rooms, to make them pleasant living spaces. I knew what I would do with the whole house, to lighten its heaviness of walls and ease the formality of the rooms, to make it a place where a family could live. But it had nothing to do with me and I didn't plan to occupy the bed I sat on. I was merely busying myself, keeping myself busy, until the afternoon would pass.

• • •

Aimless, that's what I was, especially when alone. Purposeless. There was a woman in a bar, late one May afternoon, an afternoon in late May...and what I was doing in a bar I couldn't have said. She looked married, she looked unhappy, she suited my mood. She had asked me to pass the pretzels, please. Not a pretty woman, not young, her body looked as if it had borne children, her face looked lived in. I passed the pretzels. She yawned, covering her mouth with a not-manicured hand.

"Long day," I suggested, sympathetically.

"Are there any short ones?" She smiled. "What's your name?"

"Gregor."

"Mine's Joy." She made a sound like a bark of laughter. Or a bite. "And that's a joke. What brings you in here, Greg? You don't exactly look the type."

I made up my mind. It was something to do with the way her hand emerged from the tailored cuff of her blouse, with the strong wrist. Unless her looks and clothing were entirely deceptive, she wasn't in a high-risk group. You couldn't be entirely sure, not of anyone, you can't be, but I had condoms in my wallet. Even with condoms, you can't be entirely sure, but the way I felt, a little surety was enough. "I was thinking of dinner, and a movie."

She waited, then asked the question herself. "With me?"

"If you'd like to. We could see a movie first and then eat, if you'd rather."

She didn't look me up and down but concentrated on my face, eyes. "Are you married?"

"No," I said.

She sighed. "You're lying. I can tell, I can always tell. I

167

was married, for twenty years almost, until last New Year's Eve. Isn't that a hell of a time to tell your wife you want a divorce?"

"Maybe he thought there was something symbolic about it?"

"There was. There sure as hell was. Have you ever been married?"

"No."

She munched on a pretzel and considered me. "I like you, Greg, you just bare-faced lie. And you've got sympathetic eyes. I like your eyes. So maybe we'll do that, even if you are married. Because you have to begin sometime, don't you?"

I didn't answer.

"And after all, my husband was married too, wasn't he?"

"I should warn you," I warned her, "I'm not looking for anything permanent."

"Who is, Greg? Who in the whole lousy city is?"

We never made it to the movie. We also never made it to bed. We ate and talked, drank coffee and talked—about her life, children, marriage. "I didn't expect Prince Charming, nobody in her right mind would, but he did. Not Prince Charming, and not Cinderella, exactly—more Sophia Loren, some dark Italian beauty, oversexed and overdomesticated…What do you think, Greg, are all men that stupid? Or just him?" I walked her home, to an East Village apartment, kissed her at the door for whatever good that might do, and said good-bye, good night. I walked home, uptown, along dark streets. I would have liked it if someone tried to mug me, the way I felt. But nobody rose to the bait.

26

THE LAST TEMPTATION

I could have left Mr. Theo's employ, but—

Not that I didn't think of it, not that I wasn't tempted. But I had references to consider, and if I were to simply walk out, without notice, there would be a three-year gap in my resume, too long a time to leave unexplained. Also, I was contractually bound to give him thirty days' notice, and morally bound to see him through his marriage. I could hold out, I thought. It was only a matter of waiting out the time. So I set myself aside and derived whatever pleasure I could from the comedy playing out before me.

Besides, while I didn't mind having deceived Alexis, I found I did mind having disappointed her. The expression of shame and scorn I saw in her eyes whenever I met them— that galled me. By behaving well, by impeccable behavior, I could regain the sense that I at least deserved respect.

So I stayed on, playing my part in the occasion. Like the bridegroom's, mine was a passive, enabling role. The ladies were active. I often carried in trays of tea or coffee, cakes or sandwiches, to whatever ladies were embroiled in whatever decisions needed making. Miss Sarah stayed on at the house. Alexis was often in conference with her and Mrs. Mondleigh and Mrs. Rawling in the library. The four of them worked at the production of the wedding. Mrs. Rawling for lack of time and Mrs. Mondleigh for lack of interest left the redecoration project to the two younger women. I kept to the background, kept the background running smoothly behind them.

Once again, I was carrying a tray of tea out to the library, late in an afternoon. Miss Sarah and Alexis, old friends by this period of forced intimacy, were once again at work among wallpapers and fabrics and books about color, Miss Sarah in jeans and one of Mr. Theo's old shirts, Alexis in a Laura Ashley sundress. I set the tray down on a place Alexis cleared for it. They were each at one end of the deep leather sofa.

"Thanks, Gregor," Miss Sarah said. She was the more obsessed of the two about getting everything decided before the wedding, but I assumed that she had more she wanted not to be thinking about. I moved the teacups onto their saucers and turned to leave.

"Wait a minute," Miss Sarah stopped me. "We should ask Gregor, Allie. He's got great taste. Have you seen his room? He did it all himself, I mean, designing and decorating."

"No," Alexis answered, and I could guess what she was thinking. "I've never seen his room."

Miss Sarah had no such suspicion of anyone. "It was this dingy—Victorian—rabbit warren, for servants, and Gregor's turned it into—I guess it's a suite. Would you call it a suite, Gregor?"

"Mr. Theo was very generous," I explained to Alexis.

"He transformed the whole thing, it's—You ought to see it, Allie. If it weren't Gregor's, I'd ask Theo if I could have it. You looked at the servants' quarters in the old house, didn't you, Gregor?"

"Yes."

"What did you think? You must have thought something. What would you do with them?"

She was impervious to the subtleties. I was not. "If I may, miss?" I inquired of Alexis, forcing her to look at me. Scorn and shame.

"Go right ahead."

"I'd do it—them—in white, a warm white but not too creamy. With bold colors, crayon colors. I wouldn't move any walls: the rooms themselves aren't bad, the house is well built. But at present they're depressing." I remembered. "You'll want to refurnish them. I'd do modern, wood rather than glass or metal." She nodded her head, a good girl, listening politely.

"Is there anything else?" I asked Miss Sarah.

In the kitchen, I picked up a book. I had decided to kill the time reading through Dickens, *The Pickwick Papers* to *The Mystery of Edwin Drood*. I had arrived at *David Copperfield*.

Alexis entered the kitchen, bearing the teapot. I stood up. "You should have rung."

She paid no attention to what I said or to my tone. "Is

171

it true what she's telling me? She got married? and divorced? this spring? within three weeks?"

I didn't contradict any of it.

"Gregor, she's in there—just crying. Weeping. I don't know what started it, I didn't say anything. I don't think I said anything that would start it. What can I do?"

"Talk to her like a friend, miss," I advised.

"That's no problem. She's sweet. Silly, but—I never had a little sister but I like having Sarah. What should I say?"

She had forgotten who she was speaking to, and that was a welcome change. "Say whatever seems true to you. Although…I don't think the time is right for feminist points."

She smiled unselfconsciously, nodded thoughtfully, and left. I assumed I was supposed to refill the teapot, so I put the kettle on and cleaned out the old leaves. The water came to a boil. I swished some around in the pot, poured that into the sink, and was measuring out tea when Alexis came back into the kitchen.

"Gregor, what is this?" she demanded. "Brad rescued her?"

I nodded.

"She won't tell me. What did he rescue her from? Do you know? Why *didn't* she tell him who she was?"

I shrugged and poured water.

"She's desperately unhappy, Gregor. What happened?"

I shook my head, as if to say I couldn't say. She stared at me, then picked up the teapot and went back to Miss Sarah.

I returned to my reading. Sunlight fell silently beyond the window. I turned pages.

Alexis entered and sat down facing me. She reached across to take the book out of my hands. "She's pregnant."

"Pregnant?"

"Pregnant."

I didn't know why I should be so surprised.

"She's gotten the test results. Does Brad know?"

This added a whole new dimension to the situation. "I doubt it. I don't think they've communicated in any way since she left him." This changed everything.

"The way Sarah tells it, he left her."

"Yes."

"After she told him who she was."

I related the events impartially. "She told him, he was furious, he left for work and didn't call or come back, so she moved out. Before ten thirty a.m."

She took a minute to take it in. "She doesn't want to tell him about the baby."

"Of course not."

"She says she wants to forget it ever happened. *It* being Brad."

"A baby makes that difficult."

"Well, she's not thinking very clearly," Alexis allowed. She rested her chin on her hand, waiting for whatever I would say next. I noted a distinct lack of scorn and shame on her face, and I hated to risk the question but it seemed an obvious one to ask.

"Can you ascertain how she feels about an abortion? Not in principle, but for herself."

"It's so sad, Gregor. She's so naive. What could she have done to him?"

"He's young himself. Growing up rich keeps you young."

"Tell me about it," Alexis said. She rose from the table and returned to Miss Sarah.

I didn't pick up my book. I looked out the window to the garden, walled in by buildings, and tried to imagine what Miss Sarah, pregnant, might be feeling. It was useless to spend any time being impatient with their lack of precautions. Caution hadn't characterized the affair, not at any point.

Alexis entered the kitchen but stayed across the room. I waited. "She wants you too. She asked me to ask you… Bring a cup, there's plenty of tea."

I offered her a way out. "You don't mind?"

"Mind?" I'd angered her. "What do you think I am? She's twenty, she ran off and got married, she ran off and got divorced, now she's pregnant and doesn't know what to do, and she trusts you. I'd mind if you refused."

She didn't wait for me. I got down a cup and saucer and followed her. Miss Sarah, looking about fourteen with blotchy eyes and runny nose and quivering lips, greeted me: "It just gets worse and worse. What am I going to do?" She answered herself, by wailing.

She was alone on the big sofa. I sat beside her. She wept. I put an arm around her and gathered her in, until she could bury her face against my shoulder.

I told her, "What you're going to do is cry, and when you're through with that, we'll talk." Her face moved against my jacket, in what I took to be agreement.

Alexis passed me a box of Kleenex. She poured tea into

my cup, miming sugar? milk? lemon? I nodded or shook my head.

It could almost have been our own child over whose weeping head we communicated without words; or a niece, and we the dependable adults in her world. We were for her, and against whatever that required us to be against. We were allies.

Eventually Miss Sarah drew back and blew her nose and rubbed at her eyes and looked absolutely miserable. "I feel better," she said to both of us. "It always helps to blow off steam. Gee, I'm sorry, Allie. There's no reason for me to lay all this on you."

"We're almost sisters, Sarah. Does Theo know?"

"He knows I got married. He doesn't know about the divorce, only Gregor knew that. And until today, nobody knew about——" Her voice cracked. I put the Kleenex box into her hand.

My first objective was to soothe. "Miss Sarah?"

Her reddened eyes looked at me over a tissue.

"It's not the end of the world, being pregnant. Especially not when you're rich."

Her eyes widened when I mentioned the unmentionable.

"In the first place, it can mean the best medical care, if you decide on an abortion…?"

She shook her head, absolutely not.

"In that case…You'll have control over your own money when you turn twenty-one, won't you?"

That thought cheered her.

"So you'll be all right, no matter what you decide."

"I will, won't I?" She lowered the tissue.

I think I had shocked Alexis, but I went on, regardless. "The difficult thing is to decide what you want."

"I want everything to be the way it was. It was wonderful, Allie, it was perfect. And now I wish I'd never met him."

I got her back on the rails: "I could tell your brother, and he could talk to Mr. Wycliffe."

She had started shaking her head before I finished the first conditional clause. "No, no. Don't do that. Please. You won't, will you?"

I reserved judgment.

"You don't understand Brad. He's an idealist. He means what he says."

Alexis cut in. "What I don't understand, Sarah, is why he refused to come here. You say you know he won't, but I don't understand why."

I attempted to deflect her. "Sarah," I said, "Brad must also have said he'd always love you. If I know anything about people, he must have said that too."

"But that won't matter if he doesn't think he should. If he thinks he shouldn't love me, it won't be the same, what he's said. You see," she said, "I know what he's like."

Alexis was not to be distracted. "What does he have against this house?"

Miss Sarah turned to her. "I can't tell you. You're going to marry Theo."

Alexis directed her face at me. "Gregor? What is she talking about?"

"Believe me, Mr. Theo was much maligned." I composed my face to trustworthiness.

She knew what I was doing. "Believe *you*?"

"Ask Theo, if you want to know," Sarah suggested. I

could understand her impulse to spite, but I did wish she could have restrained herself on this occasion. "He's the one you're marrying. If that's what you want. Allie," the question had just occurred to her, "is that what you want? To marry Theo? Or is it just what our parents want for the two of you?"

"Theo and I have known one another almost all of our lives," Alexis reassured her. "It's bound to be different than, say, you and Brad. We'll do fine, don't worry about me. It's what you want I'm trying to think about."

There was something each of us didn't want to have to speak of. Or think of.

"I guess," Miss Sarah said, "I want to have this baby. No, I really do. I think I need someone to love, and that's what a baby is, isn't it? It's just—I don't know how to have a baby."

"I'll take you at your word," Alexis said, "if you're sure?" Miss Sarah nodded.

"Then listen. There's my house on Lake George. You could go there. You could live there. It's winterized. You'll have to find a doctor, and I don't think you should be alone. Is there a friend who could stay with you?"

"Would you?" Miss Sarah asked.

Alexis smiled, gentle. "I think Theo might object."

I had served my purpose, and rather well I thought, so I rose from the sofa. "If you don't need me...?" I inquired, back in character.

"I guess I don't," Miss Sarah said. "Except you make me feel better, just being here. I'd like to adopt you for a brother. Gregor? How about you, you could come stay with me. Would you? Would you do that for me?"

Alexis wouldn't look at me. She wasn't going to give me any help, or hinder me in any way. I could see how it might go if I moved up to Lake George with Miss Sarah, as her resident friend: there would be daily life and childbirth classes, an intimacy rife with possibilities. I liked the girl well enough, and I was tempted. Not very tempted, and not for very long, given the long-range difficulties. "Wouldn't you be better off with a girlfriend?" I suggested.

"I guess. Yeah, I think. Besides, people would talk about us, wouldn't they? And then, after it's born—Do you think it's a boy or a girl, Alexis? I can barely wait to see it. I'd love to have a boy or a girl. This is exciting, isn't it?" she said, in wonder. "This is going to be exciting."

"Thank you, Gregor," Alexis said. There were shadings to her voice and I wondered if I had spared her the uncomfortable choice between telling all or abandoning Miss Sarah to the fate of me. Had I seized the opportunity, would that have been her deepest shame?

27

I MEET MY MATCH

Through the kitchen windows I could see how fine the morning was—spring ripening into summer, May coming to its end, daffodils and tulips gone, and roses just beginning. I was sitting at the table with the silver piled in front of me, applying polish.

"Sarah still asleep?" Mr. Theo entered from the dining room, carrying his breakfast tray. "She went to bed at ten last night. I don't know why she needs so much sleep. You don't think she's sick, do you Gregor?"

"I've given some thought to that, sir," I answered, judiciously.

He pulled out a chair, sat down, watched me. His tanned face had that sleek look, freshly shaven. "I guess Allie's working her pretty hard. And Mother too. The kid doesn't seem to have any social life, but I don't know when she'd have the time. She's not still mooning about over Wycliffe, is she? He hasn't been around, has he?"

"No, he hasn't."

"Poor kid took quite a nosedive over him. Once the wedding's behind us, her life will perk up. She can get a divorce. And that's not much more than two weeks now."

I rose, to clear his tray off the counter space I would need for the silver. He watched me over his shoulder. "Did you ever have the feeling that—like you're on a train and it's going the wrong place?"

"Are you having the traditional jitters, sir?"

"Maybe. I don't think so. If I am, they're sure not about Allie. Talk about the pleasure of deferred gratification. No, it's not that, it's—it's as if all you did was decide to step onto a train, and everything follows from its own impetus, not from yours. Did you ever?"

"Yes," I told him. "I do know what you mean." I knew better than to quote Frost to Mr. Theo or to mention my own experience of life. I also knew that even if I persuaded him to back out of the wedding, she wouldn't have me. All I would achieve, assuming I could succeed, would be Alexis's humiliation.

"I guess that's why you're not married," Mr. Theo— not a man of rich imagination—said. "That reminds me, Tiffany's should deliver the ring today. Don't let the boy go until you've checked the engraving. It should be my initials inside."

"Very good, sir." I accompanied him down the hallway, escorting him into the day.

"They asked me…They tried to sell me a set, his-and-hers rings. Why would a man wear a wedding ring?"

I opened the doors for him. "Perhaps for the same reason a woman does?"

"Not this man. Look at the day, Gregor. New York in May—I don't know why people dump on New York the way they do." The limousine awaited him, double-parked in front of the house.

I returned to the silver, listening with half an ear for the sounds of Miss Sarah, upstairs. My private thought was that she slept late because it took so long for her to cry herself to sleep. When the doorbell rang I was rinsing spoons. I went to answer it, drying my hands on the apron.

Alexis stood outside, in a little boxy suit and low-heeled shoes, tidy as a teapot. Her hair fluffed out around her face, fresh from being done by expert hands. It made me sad to see her: in not very many years' time she would be a little dumpling lady, without vanity because she had nothing to be vain about, Mrs. Theodore Mondleigh, probably an excellent mother although how she'd feel about herself as a wife I couldn't guess. "Good morning, miss," I greeted her. "I was expecting a delivery," I explained my appearance, shirtsleeves and apron. "Miss Sarah isn't awake yet. But come in."

She stayed put. "It's not Sarah I want to see."

I waited.

"Will you come for a walk with me, Gregor? I want to ask you something."

"Of course, miss."

"Don't talk to me like that today, please."

I couldn't think what she wanted of me. Most probably, to be sure I was not going to be part of her married life. "Let me leave a message for Miss Sarah, should she come downstairs. I won't be a minute—unless you'd like me to change?"

"Why should you?" Alexis asked.

I had no idea, which was why I'd asked.

"I'll wait out here. You *could* take off that apron."

We went side by side down the city street, toward the park, across the avenue and to the pond, where a few boats moved across the gilded water, little plastic *Pequod*s. By the time she sat down on a bench and I sat beside her if not with her, my discomfort had mounted to the point where I only wanted whatever it was to be over with.

I waited, noting the few wandering clouds, wondering if it was going to get hot by midday, watching the boats crossing and recrossing from cement rim to cement rim.

She was twisting her hands in her lap. I wanted to take her by the shoulders and shake her and make her look at me, and tell her, "Liberty has lots of prints suitable for females over the age of fourteen, dark Indian prints, rich colors." She looked over at me and took a breath, but that didn't enable speech.

I looked away.

"I'm having a hard time saying this," Alexis said.

I decided against sarcasm. Almost, I felt sorry for her. "Perhaps I can help. I won't be staying on with Mr. Theo after the wedding. I'll give him my notice."

"That's not—" she started. "I mean, thank you, Gregor. Theo will give you a good recommendation, I'm sure. But that's not it."

She had had all the help she was going to have from me.

"What will you do next?" she asked.

"I shouldn't have any difficulty finding a suitable position."

"Do you mind?" she wondered, in a little voice.

I did feel sorry for her. It wasn't her fault, after all; it wasn't her doing. It had all been my deliberate doing. "What is there for me to mind, miss?"

"You're right. It's none of my business."

"I didn't mean *that*, Alexis."

"Anyway, when you hear what I'm going to ask you, you'll think...I don't know what you'll think."

Did she want advice about a wedding present? Not likely, I thought, not bloody likely. Alexis was too tense. Inappropriately tense for merely asking the butler's advice about what would be welcome and tasteful. "Then what is it?"

If I'd been her, I'd have rapped me in the teeth for the patronizing tone, but she was too wrapped up in her own self-fortifying to take offense.

"I don't know how to begin." She lifted her mouth at the ends. Her eyes didn't see me. "I know, begin at the beginning. The beginning is Theo. Who doesn't love me— not sexually, if you know what I mean."

She checked to be sure I was following her. I nodded, I was following her.

"Even someone as inexperienced as I am can tell that. See, I've known him all my life, and he's—he's perfectly nice and all that, he's perfectly normal. There's nothing wrong with him. There's something wrong with me, that's the problem, but Theo can't see past his own nose where people are concerned. He's terrific about investments, really sharp, both knowledgeable and intuitive—which is a rare

183

combination—but about people…Including himself, you see. That's where the trouble is."

She watched my face for its reaction, as if she had explained everything.

"What trouble? Am I being obtuse?"

"You're not obtuse, Gregor," she admitted. "I guess, maybe I'm trying to justify what I'm going to ask you. Because as far as I can tell, you're trustworthy. I mean, even though you did try to deceive me, you've never tried blackmail. Not in any way. So you've got some idea of honor."

"Some small token, yes."

"Don't get huffy, don't—If I can't be honest with you, who can I be honest with?"

I unbent, smiled, let myself cherish her good opinion.

"You know as well as I do that with Theo, if the sex isn't—And the marriage won't have a chance if the sex isn't—"

I was beginning to guess at her purpose.

"Not that there would be a divorce or anything like that, but he'd…I don't know, we'd have separate bedrooms and things like that."

I had forgotten how strong an emotion anger is.

"If I'm going to get married, I want it to work. As a marriage." She looked at me again, pleading. "And I don't know anything about making love. Not anything."

"No," I said. "The answer is no, Alexis. I don't go out at stud."

She was embarrassed but determined. "I wasn't offering you money or gifts. I know better than that."

I didn't answer.

"Or did you mean children, getting pregnant? Because I've started taking the pill."

I didn't answer.

"But Gregor, I'm not talking about something cheap, some dirty weekend." She held me in place with a hand on my arm. "It's Memorial Day weekend; my parents are going off on someone's boat to Block Island. I thought we could—I thought we might go somewhere, for the weekend, somewhere you'd enjoy, maybe Bermuda or St. Barts? Anywhere you like. I've got my passport and you've got one, haven't you?"

She hadn't meant to insult me. "Alexis," I told her stiffly, "it's not possible."

"Why not? Theo won't know, he's going to Hilton Head. He won't even know enough to be grateful. Isn't it what you were after anyway?"

"I was after more."

"But you knew I couldn't marry you, not once I knew the truth. Unless—Gregor, you weren't planning not to tell me the truth, were you?"

I couldn't answer. I couldn't say. I didn't know.

"So what's the problem?" she asked. Dogged. "I've thought about it and—It wouldn't be degrading for you, Gregor. At least, I could be wrong, but I think you really do like me."

I didn't deny it.

"At least to some extent."

She was unsure now. I waited.

I could almost see her stiffening her resolve. "And I find you attractive." She made herself meet my eyes. "You know that as well as I do. You're very attractive."

I think I must have smiled. Well, it was good to think that I had at least troubled her.

"And I dreamed about you, it was…You lifted me down from a wagon, as if we were going to an old-fashioned dance, a square dance, and…your fingers touched my ribs, through the blouse I wore, I could feel them. I keep feeling that, how your fingers touched my ribs."

"You are trying to seduce me." I didn't tell her how she was succeeding.

"No. I'm asking you to help me out."

"The answer is still no, Alexis." *No* with more regret, with a lot more regret.

She accepted it. There was no point in staying there, so I got up. I was about five paces away when the thought struck me. "You won't ask somebody else?"

"There's nobody else to ask. I don't blame you, Gregor. I wouldn't either, if it were me."

I went on, away, slowly. Thinking. After another few paces I turned around to look at her: she sat quietly, watching the toy boats on the artificial pond. I walked back, slowly. She saw that but said nothing.

"All right," I said.

I had surprised her.

"But it has to be *my* weekend."

"But—"

I didn't reach out a hand or smile or make it easier for her in any way. "A nonnegotiable position," I said.

"Yes, of course. I can see that. I can accept that. Thank you, Gregor." She hesitated. "I think."

"I'll let you know where to meet me, late Friday afternoon. You'll be back home Monday evening." I was all practicality.

"What should I pack?"

"Whatever you usually would, for a weekend."

She nodded, swallowed. "You're awfully nice to do this, Gregor."

I could have laughed out loud. *Nice* wasn't the word most people would use, for me or for her. But I thought she was right about Mr. Theo and the chance of success for the marriage. "Listen, Alexis," I said, sitting down beside her, taking one of her cold hands in both of mine. In for a penny, in for a pound: I planned to enjoy myself; I planned for her to enjoy herself. "I want you to think about this, all the time until Friday. We're lovers, you and I—me for you and you for me. That's how it's going to be."

"But Gregor—"

The hand I held had Mr. Theo's ring on it. "I know, just for the weekend." It was a ring for a longer-fingered, brighter-nailed hand, not for the little stubby fingers I held. "For the whole, long weekend," I said.

"I'm sorry," she said, meaning what I don't know.

"You know? I don't think I am." The realization pleased me. If I could have pulled it off, we might have been quite something, Alexis and I. "You're a woman a man could give up everything for."

The words, as I spoke them, seemed true. It wasn't what I thought I'd been thinking, and they were probably false, but in the circumstances they rang true enough.

"Because of my money," she answered.

"Don't be sorry," I asked her.

She withdrew her hand. "Then it's settled." She stood

up and looked down at me. "I was going to see if Sarah wanted to go to a movie tonight. Theo's out of town on business"—which was the first I'd heard of it—"so I thought Sarah might like to."

I didn't know why she was marrying him, and I knew several reasons why she shouldn't, but that was no way to win her—if there remained any chance to win her, if that was what was hidden away in the bank-vault subconscious of my mind. I didn't think that was it, however; I thought it more likely that my pride had been pricked, and this was a chance to soothe it.

I wasn't thinking, that's the truth. *Why not? Why shouldn't I?* That was the extent of my thinking.

"Shouldn't we go back?" Alexis asked.

"You go ahead," I said. It was a limited victory but still worth savoring. "I'm going to sit here until I've gotten over the shock of your appalling proposition."

Which it was, the more I thought of it. Appalling, and rather wonderful. I was appalled, and eager.

28

MEMORIAL DAY WEEKEND

I was early at the airport and saw her come in, undistinguished in a crowd. She wore a mottled lavender suit, full-skirted, loosely jacketed; her dress bag she carried over her shoulder. The blown-dry hair, with its swept bangs, the little leather purse, the sensible shoes—her gait, like her face, was purposeful. She looked dowdy, dumpy. I wasn't disappointed. She looked like herself.

I bent to kiss her cheek, in greeting. I didn't take her bag. I had one of my own over my shoulder, and with my free hand I held her free hand. Without looking, I knew she wasn't wearing Mr. Theo's ring.

For the length of the plane trip we spoke only twice. I don't count her inquiry as we boarded, "Pittsburgh?" I'd hoped to surprise her.

After liftoff I took a little square box out of my pocket

and opened it for her. A pair of wedding rings shone gold against black velvet. "This one's yours." I gave it to her, and she slipped it onto her finger. "I didn't know if you'd want me to wear one."

"Yes, I would, please." So I put it on. Then she looked out the window, thinking her own thoughts. I read the copy of *The Atlantic* I'd bought in the airport. She didn't seem tense, I was at ease: we could have been a married couple.

Somewhere high over Pennsylvania she turned to me. "Gregor?" Worried, apologetic. "I should have asked before, I'm sorry. About an HIV test."

So she had thought of it. I was relieved to know that. "I had one a couple of months ago," I told her. "I haven't had a sexual encounter in the last six months. I've never been promiscuous, never knowingly slept with a high-risk person, but there's always a chance. You have to know that. As far as I know I'm healthy."

"And I'm a virgin who's never had a blood transfusion," she told me, and turned back to the window.

She trusted me. She was right to, but…Despite everything, she took me at my word, she knew she could take me at my word.

Alexis interrupted my thoughts by turning around again, to ask, "Not for six months? But I thought men—?"

"That's boys," I said, and she laughed, pleased.

The suite also surprised her. She took in the basket of fruit, the flowers, the whole wide living room with floor-to-ceiling windows, the city spread at her feet. Our luggage had been set down in the foyer.

She wandered—opening a door to find a kitchen, another door to a bedroom, back across the thick carpeting to another door and another bedroom. I watched her. "It's too much, Gregor, too expensive. And the car too."

"You said you'd leave the arrangements to me," I reminded her across the width of the room.

"But you can't—"

"All right, a financial disclosure. A limited financial disclosure." I took off my jacket while I spoke, to hang it in the coat closet. "I make a very good salary and have no living expenses. That's one of the benefits of domestic service, you know." I turned back to her. "I can afford anything I want for this weekend, Alexis."

"But two bedrooms? Why two bedrooms?"

"I didn't know—" This I wasn't sure how to say. "It doesn't matter that much to me. You don't *have* to, if you don't want to. If you want to change your mind."

I had amused her. She answered me patiently. "Usually I think about things for a long time before I make up my mind. So I don't often change it. I'm too old to be *that* young, Gregor."

"So you haven't changed your mind about this."

"No," she said.

"Ah," I said.

"Have you?"

"Me? Why should I?" An evasive answer, but I couldn't explain a growing sense of apprehension.

"How would I know? I don't know anything about

men, you know that. I don't know all that much about you, either."

"Well then, what kind of restau—?" but she spoke at the same time "Should I change into—?"

"You go ahead," she instructed me.

"I was wondering where you'd like to eat."

"Anything is fine. Whatever you like. I'm not very hungry."

She was not enjoying herself. "Well," I suggested, "if you're not hungry. The question is…We could get it over with now. Would you prefer that?"

Her laughter bubbled up, like a girl's. There was no nervousness in it, just appreciation of the silly clumsiness—hers and mine, and whatever was indigenous to our situation. I moved toward her, where she stood with her chin lifted.

"It's what lovers would do, what lovers do," I said, "before they've even unpacked."

I was hidden behind the morning newspaper when she came out of the bedroom. I lowered the paper to just below my eyes: she wasn't the kind of woman who scurried into the bathroom to make herself up, make herself presentable. She had wrapped the hotel bathrobe about herself and bumbled out for a cup of coffee, which I poured for her. She smiled vaguely at me; I mattered less than her own thoughts. I raised the paper again, to give her privacy. Her hair was tumbled, her skin glowed, and the thick bathrobe was not flattering. I smiled to myself: Alexis had a full-fleshed body, round arms and breasts, thick haunches, but she was no dumpling. A Renoir, I thought, or Titian. She swam, she'd told me; she walked a lot when she was in the country. How did I keep in such good shape? she wondered. "Lucky genes," I'd told her, "and housework."

I had the paper up but I wasn't reading. "Gregor?" Alexis asked. I lowered it.

"Did you mean what you said?"

What had I said? I wondered. I could account for most of the time but not all. "When?" I asked, wary.

She lifted her face to laugh at me. "We're lovers now, you don't have to handle me like old crystal. You don't have to handle me now, Gregor." She stared at me. "Do I look like that too?"

"Like what?"

"I'm not sure—so plumped out, maybe. Smug?"

Well, she did. That was it, exactly. "I'm afraid so."

"And did you mean it?" she asked again, breaking a roll, buttering it. "As to when, I'm not sure, I think it was before we had supper. And how did you know to stock the refrigerator with sandwich meats and cheeses? No, don't tell me."

"What did I say?" I asked.

She studied the roll in her hands. "You said 'lovely.'"

I remembered: I had held her hair back from her face, to frame her face with my hands; her little hands had been on my cheeks, at the time, one thumb smooth as water across my lower lip; her hair had been spread across the pillow and I saw what my hands had uncovered. For a minute, I was transfixed, immobilized. "Lovely," I said. Alexis had a Renaissance forehead, broad and oval and slightly domed.

Her eyebrows were a dark curve over deep eyes and under that forehead her face had character, symmetry. She wasn't a beauty, Alexis, but she was lovely.

"Or is that just something men say?" she asked.

I folded the paper up. "Your forehead," I began. "I don't know where you have your hair styled, but you should sue them," I began. "I could show you in a mirror."

"I'm not ready for a mirror. I haven't washed my face. Or brushed my teeth, either. Do you mind?"

I didn't mind. "Neither have I."

"What do you think I should do?" she asked. "With my hair."

I didn't have to stop to think. "Grow it long. Wear it up, away from your face, full, but not piled high, just back." She was laughing at me again. "And baroque pearl earrings," I completed the picture.

Laughing, she asked, "Gregor, what are we going to do?"

"Do?" I was reasonably sure she didn't mean what a foolishly hopeful man might have hoped.

"We can't make love all day. Can we?"

"We could, but…I thought, there are a couple of interesting museums, I've got tickets to the symphony tonight, there's a zoo, there's Fallingwater…"

"You know Pittsburgh," she announced her discovery. I didn't deny it. "Did you live here?"

"Once." I distracted her by getting up. "I'm going to have a shower." I kissed her and felt her hand once again on my cheek.

"Am I supposed to feel as if I really know you now?"

"If even the way someone kisses you tells you a lot about him, or her…"

"Then I have you now."

"You have me now."

"And you have me," she realized.

"Only, I never would have guessed you'd be so talky," I said. "No, that's not a criticism."

She had twisted around in her chair, to look at me. "Am I supposed to feel *tristesse*?" she asked. "I don't."

"Good," I said. "Thank you. Now—"

"Nobody tells you," Alexis interrupted me. "How messy it is," she answered my expression. "Like—like mud pies? Is that why nobody tells you? Because it's messy and messy is—Or babies too, either, nobody tells you how messy they are. But I like that about things. I like them being messy, like playing in the mud. I like them real."

"Even with the flawed beginning?" I inquired.

Her porcelain cheeks flushed but she didn't drop her glance. "Not flawed. Just…really awkward. And as long as they finish up all right…"

"And they did?" I inquired.

"How dumb do you think I am, Gregor?" she asked me. "You know as well as I do that they—things—It's just not like the movies," she said. "It's *real*."

What we did—the concert, meals, the Carnegie, a drive out to Rolling Rock to tour Fallingwater, the zoo, a Sunday afternoon drive west along the Ohio, and always return-ing to the hotel, to one another—what we did, which I remember vividly, is less vivid in my memory than the talking. The woman talked. Not empty chatter but a barrage of ideas and questions, as if she wanted our minds to achieve the easier intimacy of our bodies. Not even separate but equal, no, she'd raise her head from my naked chest, while my blood was still thudding along, to ask a question. Sometimes it would be direct: "What do you think about the possibility of extraterrestial life, never mind science fiction fantasy, but as an objective possibility?" "How would you go about reducing the deficit?" Sometimes, as I was slipping into satisfied slumber, she would rouse me: "Plato, in the *Symposium*, has Aristophanes argue that men and women were originally one body that got separated." I would shift up on the pillow and guess, "You feel as if there is something to that idea? That's the way you feel right now?"

"You're telling me it's temporary, a temporary euphoria. But I know that."

"Although it's only humans who make love face to face as standard practice," I realized.

"Is that true? What about monkeys, apes: do you know anything about their sexual practices? I don't."

As we drove out of town towards Fallingwater, through lush western Pennsylvania foliage, the car humming along the sweet curves of the road, she asked, "Gregor? Why do people take sex so seriously? Make it so serious."

"What do you mean?"

"They do, in books, movies—Don't look like that at me. If you don't have actual experience, you have to get your information somewhere."

"There's recreational sex, that's an accepted phrase."

"No, I don't mean that. Why are you so touchy? Are you feeling defensive? Don't, I didn't mean you. And sex-for-love, married sex too, it's always shown as serious, serious business, earnest, charged with significance."

"What do you think it is?"

"I think it's fun. No, that's sloppy, I mean…glad. Joyous." She reached over to put her hand on the back of my neck. "It's really something, isn't it, Gregor?"

I wished she had told me that in the darkness of our bed, where I could have closed my eyes in silent celebration. "That's you, Alexis," I told her.

"Oh good," she said.

And me, I thought, *us*.

"If you had strong religious impulses, you'd approach God the same way, I bet," I told her.

"Like the singing nun?"

I laughed. I couldn't plumb the depths of her. I had sent down my line but it hadn't yet touched bottom.

"There's something wrong with the way we think about God, isn't there?" Alexis said then. "Do you know anything about the Eastern religions?"

She talked about her family, and her life. In that respect at least she was predictable. "I never fit in, never felt comfortable, with anyone, with any situation. Especially when I was a kid. Adulthood is easier, don't you think?"

I thought. I opened my mouth to comment.

Alexis said, "I never knew what I was supposed to say, what anyone wanted from me—except my parents, and they're devoted to me. Disappointed, but devoted. You know how parents are? Mine are just…more so. They don't have any friends, just each other. But that's enough for them."

"Do you? Have friends?"

"A few, a couple of good friends, women. From schools, so they're scattered all over the map. I don't make friends easily, I don't attract them, and then, once you've got your academic interests focused, you tend to run into the same people so…Do you?"

"No," I said.

"There's me," she offered. "You know, I've told you all about my life. Took about ten minutes, didn't it?"

"At least twenty."

"But you don't tell anything. I'm not criticizing, Gregor, just observing."

We were in the car, driving west along the Ohio River Boulevard, which runs beside the river. It was Sunday afternoon, and most businesses were closed along the highway, in the villages. Near Ambridge, I slowed to point out the mill, the long, low cement-colored buildings splayed along the river's edge, windowless, flat-roofed. Row on row of cars filled the parking lots spread around it. The mill loomed. I turned off the Boulevard to drive down the main street of town. Flat plate-glass windows over gray sidewalks, neon signs grayed by grit, a few men out on the Sunday street corners, gray-green asphalt siding on the houses lined up along hilly side streets—I could only take so much of it, and we headed up, away from the river, into the hills, to the country inn where we were having dinner. "You grew up here," she guessed.

"Yes."

"Is your family still here?"

"Yes."

"I don't understand. But you don't want me to, do you?"

On the way back, I pulled to the side of the road on a hill high above the river. The sky had darkened over the bluff opposite, and the river looked like a broad flow of oil. Now the bluff was only a hunched dark mass, but I remembered.

"There used to be—They used to pour the slag down over there, across the river. It was like a waterfall, golden, flowing. They tipped it out of cauldrons; it was like lava. Beautiful."

"A golden river, like a fairy tale." She sat with her legs tucked under her, curled on the seat. The seat was deep enough, she was little enough to curl up on it. "Isn't there a fairy tale, 'King of the Golden River'?"

"It was no river," I said, reminding which one of us I'm not sure. "Slag runs at well over nine hundred degrees. Centigrade. I've seen a man burn his thumb off, in a second's carelessness." And heard him. And smelled it.

"You're showing me this as a metaphor," Alexis said. She reached over; her little fingers traced my cheekbone, my eyebrow. "You worked in the mills."

I nodded.

"You don't look like a millworker."

"Appearances are deceptive."

"But you must have quit when you were young, eighteen."

"How do you know?"

"You said you left home fifteen years ago. Fifteen from thirty-three is eighteen. Why did you?"

I hesitated.

"I don't have any right, Gregor," she said. "I understand."

I thought of that golden river, running down. It seemed to fall into the black water and disappear; in fact, it never reached the river but cooled like candle wax on the land below. "I might never have," I told her, "except circumstances combined on me," I said. "Ganged up. You know how sometimes circumstances do that?" She nodded, she did know. "I had a sister. I'm not sure you can understand this, without having had a sister or brother, but…she was my sister. She was wild, she ran wild, she was always self-destructive, that was her character. With schools, with our parents, she was always at odds with the world, always. Drugs were inevitable, I guess, but when I tried to tell my parents—She'd outgrow it, that was their line, nothing to get upset about. Just Lisa's life. They wouldn't be told, there was nothing I could tell them—they'd known a lot of people who were wild when they were young, and they all outgrew it—until it was too late, and then they just slapped her into an institution."

"I'm sorry," Alexis said, and meant it. "You must have been angry—I know, that's not the half of it. Do you keep in touch with them?"

"Nothing your parents would accept as keeping in touch."

"What other circumstances did you mean?" she asked. "You said a combination of circumstances."

I shrugged. The slag fell over the bluff; I could remember the roar of it, but the sound didn't carry across the river and up to our vantage point. "There was a girl and she got pregnant. I took all the cash I could get my hands on and left the country. Went to Europe. It seemed to me that if you had money you had everything, and if you didn't ..... Do you have any idea what it's like to work as hard as you can and barely get by? I didn't see why—" I could hear the echoes of old despair in my voice and tried to lighten it. "I thought there wasn't any real difference in people, so I decided to find out what I could do for myself. Get for myself."

"What became of the girl?"

"I don't know." To her silence, I said, "That bothers you. If it matters, it bothered me too."

"Not enough to do anything, apparently."

"You asked me," I pointed out to her.

"I guess I wanted to hear something different—a solitary orphan's sad tale. Where you didn't...hurt people."

"I did as little of that as I could. My parents have two sons left, to look after them."

"And when you were abroad...?"

"I started out doing anything, just to survive. I didn't have any plans, just – surviving. Worked on the docks, shipped around the Mediterranean a little. I worked in a fish cannery in France and picked grapes and ended up bartending in London. I got along. That's where I decided to get the papers for domestic service, London."

"So you could live in the style you wanted to. Learn firsthand how the rich live. So you could do a good imitation. It's all right, Gregor, I'm just telling myself the truth. What you're looking for is to find someone—"

"To marry me," I reminded her. "My intentions are honorable."

She didn't bother quarreling with that. "I almost wish you luck," she said. "You won't mind living off your wife's money?"

I liked the way she assumed I would succeed. "I would. I wouldn't stand for it. It would have to be what's mine is yours, what's yours is mine."

She was too kind to mock me.

"The great thing about Theo," Alexis said, "is he's not marrying me for my money. There's no question of that. It's a danger, you know. People look at you—at me—and see this marriageable trust fund. I used to see it happening, 'Alexis Rawling, she's an only child and there's all this money.' I couldn't really tell, nobody actually gets dollar signs in their eyes, but...I couldn't ever be sure. The only way to find out for sure would be to take on a whole new identity, what Sarah did, now I think of it. And look what happened to her. So I know that Theo isn't marrying me for my money."

"Not in the accepted sense."

"Don't be angry," she said.

"The only person I could be angry with is myself."

"Gregor, if I thought you loved me, I'd be upset. I would. I'd feel like I'd taken advantage of you."

"You haven't," I promised her.

"Because I'm pretty happy, right now," she told me. "Let's go home."

"Home?" I was almost tempted.

"All right, back. To the hotel. To bed."

"Women are such realists." I laughed.

"Somebody has to be."

• • •

The plane ride back to New York was no more conversational than the ride out. She removed her ring and returned it to me. I removed mine and put both into my pocket.

"So you must have changed your name and all," Alexis said.

"In the time-honored tradition." I had the window seat. Sunlight gilded the tops of the clouds.

"I'd like to have the nerve to do that. To make a whole new life as a whole new person, and find out who I really am."

"It doesn't work that way."

"Don't disillusion me. So it *was* Rostov, like in *War and Peace*. That's why Rostov."

I took her hand, then let it go. "The trouble with intelligent women is that eventually they figure things out."

She wasn't to be distracted. "But you'd never have me without my money. I'm not blaming you."

I put her into a taxi and watched it pull away. Then the taxi stopped, backed up. She rolled down her window. "I didn't say thank you. Thank you, Gregor."

"It was a pleasure."

"It's Gregor like in Kafka, isn't it?"

She made me laugh, tying up all the loose ends like that. "'Gregor Samsa awoke one morning to find himself turned into a giant beetle,'" I quoted, for her satisfaction.

"I like you, Gregor Rostov," she said, and reached through the open window to shake my hand.

"I'm a fraud," I reminded her. "And you're getting married in twelve days."

"Thirteen," she corrected me. That time the taxi drove away without stopping.

29

THE TRIUMPH OF LOVE

If I'd known, or even suspected…

If I'd had the slightest idea what the risk was, I would never have agreed to it, never gone off for the weekend, never have slept with her. Not having known, or suspected, I reverted to the pagan custom of not naming. I could have lost her and never been the wiser, which was preferable to losing her and being the wiser. It had nothing to do with telling her. It had everything to do with telling myself the name. To name the demon is to summon him forth. Or her.

It was too late, of course, and I knew it.

Luckily, there were diversions. There was much to be done, in preparation for and celebration of events. A wardrobe to get ready, groomsman gifts to be engraved and wrapped, wedding presents to receive and log in, then pack up to be sent out to Connecticut. There was the house to

keep and a final family dinner to look forward to. There
was the social calendar to be kept abreast of. I forwent my
usual days off. Mr. Theo—himself occupied with preparing his office for an extended absence, with preparing an
itinerary where he could be reached immediately in case
of urgency—gratefully offered me the use of the house
while I was settling on my next employment. Miss Sarah
had undertaken me as adviser and confidant. Together we
considered whether it was necessary for her to withdraw to
Lake George, and how the solitude might affect her, and
who might share it with her. We discussed what she might
do after the baby was born, where she might live, and in
what style. We talked about doctors, natural childbirth
classes, nutrition, layettes.

With so much to do, the days passed.

As I was rolling out the puff pastry which would be
the final course of my final dinner, the doorbell summoned
me. The house was empty. I had no choice but to answer
the door, probably to receive some last-minute gift, which
would have to be hastily sent to the country to take its
place in the display rooms, an inconvenience to everyone.

Brad Wycliffe waited outside. He wore office dress, a
gray suit with deep-blue pinstripes, a striped tie, a clean-
shaven face.

"Gregor." He was stern, manly.

"Sir?" I was imperturbable.

"Is my wife at home?"

I placed myself in the center of the open door. "She's
not here."

"I called Connecticut," he told me. "They told me she's
staying with her brother."

"She's out."

He looked over my shoulder. There was no reason for him to believe me. "Out where? Out with who?"

"Out shopping with Miss Rawling."

There was no sound, no movement for him to catch inside the house. "When do you expect her back?"

I added a few hours, thinking that it would give Miss Sarah time to think. "Around five."

Mr. Wycliffe stepped back and eyed me suspiciously.

"If there's nothing else, sir?"

He charged at me and pushed. I considered having the battle but decided against it. "I'll just see for myself," he announced, hurtling past me.

I waited by the inner door while he satisfied himself, downstairs, upstairs, in my lady's chamber.

"All right, she's not here," he said, from the landing. "So I'll wait."

I maintained motionless disapproval. His face had the sullen righteousness of youth aggrieved, and I wondered what had brought him here. He might as well, I thought, meet Miss Sarah here as elsewhere. It would do her good to see him in the house he'd sworn never to enter. "Very good, sir."

"And I'll have coffee, while I'm waiting."

"Very good."

I withdrew, to grind coffee and heat water. I was pouring water through the top of the Chemex when Mr. Wycliffe stormed into the kitchen, brandishing a small white bottle. He rattled the bottle at me. "I found these in her room. Do you know what they are?"

"No, sir."

"Vitamins," he announced.

"Vitamins," I echoed.

"Maternity vitamins." He rattled them again. "She's pregnant, isn't she? Don't bother lying, Gregor, you were in on the game all along. I'm sure she's told you. *I'm* the one she couldn't be bothered to tell."

He sat down and slammed the bottle on the table. "A doctor's office called this morning. My secretary took the message—my *secretary*." His fists were clenched. "What the hell am I supposed to do now?"

"Sir?"

I poured coffee and set it down before him. "Cream?" He shook his head. "Sugar?" He shook his head again, jaw clenched.

"It was some nurse, calling about prenatal classes. I must have sounded like a real chump. I had no idea what she was talking about. The nurse, she must have thought... But you knew, didn't you?"

"I knew." What I didn't know was how the doctor knew to call Mr. Wycliffe.

He took that further blow to his pride. He sipped his coffee and felt worse. "What are they off shopping for, bassinets? Diapers? Baby blankets?"

"They're picking up the bridesmaids' gifts, Miss Rawling's stationery, Miss Sarah's shoes."

"I'll have to take her back now."

I poured myself a cup of coffee and put the marble slab with pastry on it back into the refrigerator, selecting my words. "Take her back?"

"Well, she's pregnant, I don't have any choice. Pregnant with my child. That at least I'm sure of."

"Congratulations," I offered.

"Don't get funny with me." He drank again. "I put her on a pedestal, I wanted to give her everything, and she was just—laughing at me. I bet you got a good laugh out of it too. But a man doesn't abandon a pregnant wife, and Sarah's so young. Immature. She didn't even leave me a note; she never called to say where she was, nothing. She could never raise a child. You've seen the irresponsible way she acts."

"Ah, yes," I mumbled into my coffee.

"So I have to take her back. Do you know what harebrained scheme she's cooking up now?"

"You'll have to ask her about that yourself."

"Yeah, I guess so." He didn't sound entirely displeased at the prospect. My guess was that he welcomed this excuse for confrontation, for a meeting. "It's not the way I thought things would turn out."

"It never is," I assured him.

"Look, Gregor"—his anger had spent itself—"go ahead with whatever it is you were doing. I'm just going to wait."

I removed the marble pastry slab from the refrigerator and went back to rolling out a circle of dough.

"When is this wedding anyway?"

"The day after tomorrow. Tonight's a family dinner, the two families." I spoke with my back to him. "Tomorrow's the rehearsal dinner, at the Club. In Connecticut. Then the wedding, Saturday."

"I guess I'll be making an appearance, since I'm a member of the family now. I guess I'll be eating a little more crow. I tell you frankly, Teddy Mondleigh is not my idea of what I want in a brother-in-law, and I can just imagine the kind of girl he's marrying. Some bundle of sticks with blood so blue you could dye cloth with it, that's for marriage. For pleasure—he'll take that where he finds them, and you can be sure he'll find them. You wouldn't catch him marrying for love. And if I had it to do again… If only Sarah hadn't gotten pregnant."

I forbore all the obvious responses. Carefully, I moved the rolled dough from the marble slab onto a baking tray. I took the remainder from the refrigerator and began rolling it out. "You know," I said, looking at the young man over my shoulder, "I don't think I'd tell Miss Sarah I felt that way."

"And how am I supposed to feel, after the way she tricked me?"

I took it as a genuine question, and I think it might have been. "It's not every man who could keep something like that to himself."

"Oh, I can keep my own counsel. If it comes to that. What I don't like is being forced into a lie. That puts me on her level."

I didn't argue the point. I left him to his own thoughts and concentrated on my dough.

When we heard doors opening, he was out of his chair like a shot and ahead of me down the hall. I followed quickly.

Alexis entered first, and she gave me the quick, inattentive smile she had made a recent habit of. Miss Sarah was behind her and saw only the young man. "Brad?"

"I forgot how—" he said, stock-still, blocking all movement.

"Brad," she said. Her face answered any doubts I might have had. His face should have answered all of hers.

"Come on, Sarah, let's go home," he said. "I'm taking you home."

Alexis looked at me. I tried to appear reassuring.

"You're what?" Miss Sarah said. "I won't. I have my life planned out."

"Without me in it."

"You said you were never setting foot in this house. You *said*."

"I know where I am," he told her. He'd have done better to simply take her into his arms, but he was too young to know that.

"So?" she demanded.

"So...so...So you're my wife and you're—you're my wife." He turned to Alexis, without interest, then focused his hostility on me. "Can I talk to my wife in private?"

"What if I don't want to?"

Alexis tried reason. "Shouldn't you at least hear what he has to say?"

"He doesn't mean what he says."

Once he'd achieved the right forceful tone, Mr. Wycliffe carried on with it. He took shopping bags out of Miss Sarah's hands and passed them to me. "Take these, Gregor. We"—he stood before her, determined—"are going to have a talk."

Miss Sarah's cheeks were pink and her eyes sparkled. She would enjoy the occasion, however it went. "Oh, all right."

I turned around to return to the kitchen. Alexis followed me. Once she realized we were alone together, she became uncomfortable.

"You must be tired," I offered. "I've got fresh coffee."

"Thank you. What are you making?"

"Puff pastry." I poured out coffee and handed her the cup. She didn't sit down. "For tonight. For *pithiviers*."

Then she did sit down. I remained standing, took the bowl of chilled filling out of the refrigerator, took up a wooden spoon.

"I was afraid it was for beef Wellington," Alexis said.

"Only gluttons eat beef Wellington."

"No, only gluttons eat it more than once," she corrected me. I didn't turn around to see if she was in fact smiling. It was enough to hear that she might be. "It's the kind of thing—you have to try it once in your life."

I shaped the filling, set the top pastry round over it.

"He knows, doesn't he?" she asked.

I took a little knife, to scallop the sides. "Who?"

"Brad."

"Knows what?" I turned the baking sheet, cutting scallops.

"That she's pregnant. How did he find out?"

"Apparently, the obstetrician's office called to set up childbirth classes. He was furious."

"That means she gave them his name. And address."

"The office address," I pointed out.

"I wonder why."

"She's divorced him," I reminded her.

"But that was before she knew about the baby. Now it might be different. And if he was only looking for an excuse…Men need an excuse to justify love."

"And women use love as an excuse to justify any action."

I shouldn't have said that. I knew it, but I said it anyway.

"I don't love him, Gregor; you know that."

But I hadn't known if she knew it.

"It was never love I was looking for," she said.

"What were you looking for?"

"Oh, who knows," and she smiled at me. "Some reason to get out of bed in the morning."

Then we were laughing, both of us. Miss Sarah burst into the room. "What am I going to do, Allie?"

Immediately, she had all of Alexis's attention. "Did you tell him about the baby?"

"No—so maybe he does love me? But I don't know if I still love him. Nothing like I'm going to love the baby."

"About the divorce, Miss Sarah," I asked. "Did you tell him about the divorce?"

"That's none of his business, if he couldn't be bothered to be around." She thought. "I told the doctor Brad is the father. Now I wish I hadn't. What should I do?"

She was asking Alexis to decide for her. Alexis obliged. "Why don't you and Brad go up to Lake George. Spend some time together, tell each other the truth. Give yourselves a chance."

"Oh," Miss Sarah breathed. "Oh, Allie. That's so smart. You do love Theo after all, don't you? You must, or how could you know that?" She leaned down and kissed Alexis on the cheek. I could have done the same. I looked at Alexis's mouth and longed for the right to kiss her.

"There's going to be one more at dinner, Gregor," Miss Sarah told me. "I bet Mummy'll be surprised. And Daddy'll be furious. I can barely wait to tell them."

Alexis looked after her, even after the door had swung shut. "With any luck—"

"Alexis, is that what you think?" My guard was ready to go down at the slightest glimmer of hope.

"I don't know what I think." She sounded tired, and impatient with me. She rose from the table. "There's tonight's dinner, and the rehearsal tomorrow, another dinner, then a luncheon, then the wedding."

I didn't know who she was reminding about that. "And then?" I asked.

"And then the rest of my life, I guess. What about you?"

"I'll take a few weeks' vacation, then look for another position. I'll be gone before you get back."

"I've asked Theo to find a couple to replace you," Alexis said. If she'd been wearing gloves, she'd have been drawing them onto her hands. "I'll see myself out, Gregor. I know you have a lot to do."

"Yes, miss," I answered. I knew I was in a trap of my own devising, the Minotaur walled into a labyrinth of my own design. Thinking I was so clever. But how was I supposed to know I would love her?

30

TOASTING MARRIAGE

After that long last dinner, four long courses long, I served coffee and set out glasses for champagne. It seemed to me that I had begun this meal at the dawn of time and there was an eon yet to run before its end.

I poured Dom Pérignon into the long-stemmed crystal glasses and gave the table a final glance, assuring myself that now I could withdraw. The candles burned, the linens gleamed, and the few remaining pieces of silver shone. The company was seated in pairs. Mr. Theo, plump with bon-homie and self-satisfaction, had the head of the table with Alexis on his right. Beside her, her father and mother wore the expressions of a couple whose begonia has taken first prize at a show—expressions of hard work justly rewarded in this best of all possible worlds. They frequently caught one another's eye and touched hands and were glad together.

The Mondleighs shared no such gestures. He faced his son, down the length of the table, sternly satisfied, allowing perhaps himself and certainly his son no greater pleasure in the occasion, a weighty presence, stabilizing. His wife shone quietly at his side, despite his efforts to dampen her spirits. She seemed to be in a world of her own; she had smiled her greeting to me, incandescent as a bride.

Miss Sarah and Mr. Wycliffe were fully occupied, on this their first public appearance, with being taken as acknowledged adults. They concealed their affection and appetite for one another and gave most of their attention to Mr. Mondleigh, as the most significant person at the table.

I finished pouring and set the champagne bottle down on the sideboard. It had been a long evening. "Take a glass for yourself, Gregor," said Mr. Theo.

A generous gesture. I took a glass, filled it, and waited. Mr. Theo stood up.

"This is the last quiet time we'll have together, so I want to take the occasion to propose a toast, to my bride." He raised his glass and we all drank to Alexis. "And to her parents"—they were surprised and pleased—"and all happiness to you, Sarah," he concluded. He sat down again. The three toasts had emptied his glass and depleted others; I took up a bottle and filled them all again, as Mr. Mondleigh tapped with his spoon on his water goblet.

"I didn't mean to initiate a round, Dad," Mr. Theo said. "You don't have to—"

"I want to," Mr. Mondleigh silenced his son. He stood. He cleared his throat. "Life," he announced, "doesn't usually come up to expectations, but this occasion fulfills my hopes. I propose a toast to the bride and groom."

We drank to the bride and groom.

Mr. Rawling wanted a turn. He pushed his chair back and stood, his glass raised in one hand, his wife's hand held in the other. "I'll keep it simple because—because it seems simple to me. Anyone who doesn't know how much Allie means to her mother and me doesn't know much of anything. So we want to toast Theo, our son-to-be, and also neighbor-to-be, golf partner—and maybe even investment counselor. We wouldn't give her over to just anyone, Theo." Mrs. Rawling's head nodded in vigorous agreement.

We drank to Mr. Theo. Mr. Rawling sat down. I went around topping up glasses as conversation recommenced, with Mrs. Rawling at once asking Mr. Theo about an usher's family and Mr. Mondleigh grilling Mr. Wycliffe in yet more detail about his law firm. When Mrs. Mondleigh tapped her spoon against her goblet, conversation didn't falter. She tapped again. I picked up my own glass from the sideboard.

Mrs. Mondleigh continued her gentle tapping.

"What are you doing?" Miss Sarah asked. "Mother? Women aren't supposed to—"

"Pipe down, Sarah," Mr. Theo said. "This is the era of equality."

"Don't encourage her, Theo," Mr. Mondleigh told his son.

"Am I going to have to make a toast?" Mrs. Rawling demanded. "Nobody said anything about the mother of the bride making a toast."

Mrs. Mondleigh tapped again.

"Whatever you're thinking of, Elaine," Mr. Mondleigh said, "I'd be grateful if you'd change your mind."

"Go ahead, Mother, if you want to," Mr. Theo exhorted.

"I only want to…" Mrs. Mondleigh began. They finished the sentence for her.

"Embarrass me," Miss Sarah said.

"Make a toast," Mr. Theo said. "And why shouldn't she?" he demanded of his father.

"Well, get on with it, if you must," Mr. Mondleigh said. "Stand *up*."

Mrs. Mondleigh stood. She raised her glass. "I want to propose a toast to…"

"The bridal couple, we know that, you didn't have to make such a production out of it. Or did you want to include Sarah and her young man too?"

"Brad, his name is Brad," Miss Sarah told her father. "To Brad, Mother?"

"A toast to love and marriage," Mrs. Rawling suggested. "Is that what you were thinking?"

"I'll drink to that." Mr. Rawling raised his glass. Glasses around the table were raised and drunk from.

"That wasn't what…That wasn't my toast," Mrs. Mondleigh said.

"What *is* it then?" her husband asked.

"About how Theo's right, it's the last private time, and with Sarah's news…her good news…"

"Coming like a bolt out of the blue," her husband finished for her. "I know, Elaine, I know just what you mean. No offense, young man," he told Mr. Wycliffe, "you look presentable to me."

It was tears that sparkled in Mrs. Mondleigh's eyes. She didn't look at anyone. Tears sparkled on her cheeks. "I don't know what I did, that my whole family thinks it owns…I must have done something. Wrong. Mustn't I? Sarah? Theo? That's why I want to leave. After the wedding, of course."

"What do you mean?" Mr. Mondleigh demanded.

"I mean leave home, David, leave you, and live..."

"Just say what you mean, Elaine, and sit down."

"Now Sarah's married, and Theo's getting married..."

"What the hell is going on?" He pulled her back down into her seat. "What the hell do you think you're doing?"

There was a silence.

"Is she drunk?" Mr. Wycliffe asked Miss Sarah.

"Mother," Mr. Theo scolded, "this isn't the time or the place, even if you're serious—"

"It's all right, Theo," Alexis said.

"No, it is not all right." His nostrils flared.

Mr. Mondleigh sat absolutely still, jaw clenched.

"Mummy's never done anything like this before in her life," Miss Sarah told her husband. "She doesn't drink, Brad. So don't ever say that again."

"Well," Mrs. Rawling said. "I think it's time we said good evening," she announced. She folded her napkin and set it on the table. "Tomorrow's a busy day."

"I'm sorry, Theo," Mrs. Mondleigh said.

"What kind of a joke is this?" her husband asked.

"It's not a joke, David. And don't think I'm crying because I'm upset. I'm crying because..."

There was a silence.

"Finish your sentence, woman. We're all waiting, if you notice."

"Mrs. Mondleigh," Alexis asked, "are you all right?"

Mrs. Mondleigh nodded tearily. "I hope you won't think I'm trying to ruin your day, dear."

Mr. Wycliffe pushed back his chair. "I'm going home."

"Allie? Martin?" Mrs. Rawling asked brightly. "We should be going too. It was a lovely dinner, Theo."

"I hope you're not upset," Mrs. Mondleigh apologized to all.

"And I hope you're satisfied," her husband answered. "You needn't think I'll give you a divorce."

"What if the young people are right about…the real bonds. They may all be in the heart. Do you ever wonder?"

"Sarah? Are you coming with me?"

"Allie? You'd better go with your parents."

"We've been divorced for…years, my dear. And you never even knew it."

"That's ridiculous. That sounds like some book. Or some soap opera. You don't mean it, you know you don't. I don't know what's gotten into you. What's gotten into you? You'd be ludicrous, a woman like you, at your age, walking out on me, the single life at your age—It would be ludicrous. You're too sensible for that. I've always admired your good sense, and I can't believe you'd do something so out of character. I think you need a vacation, that's all. You always wanted to go to Mexico, didn't you? You could go to Mexico. For a month. Or a season. Take Sarah, if she'd like to go, she looks peaky. I'm worried about you, Elaine. I am. You don't have to speak—here, here's my handkerchief; there you go—just shake your head if I'm right. If you didn't mean it. If it's just some—mood, just shake your—I *thought* so."

He looked around but I was the only one left in the dining room.

31

THE BRIDEGROOM

The Mercedes waited in front of the house. I put Mr. Theo's suitcase into the trunk, which closed with the satisfying sound of heavy steel perfectly articulated.

Mr. Theo looked all around him, raised his face to the sun, breathed in deeply. "Well," he announced. "This is it." He descended to the sidewalk. "You're sure I can't persuade you? I know Allie has some bee in her bonnet about a couple, but you're getting married too, aren't you? So you'll be a couple."

"I'm sure, sir," I answered. "It's time for a change."

"I won't try to persuade you." He held out his hand, and I shook it. "Wish me luck, Gregor."

"It seems to me you already have the luck, sir."

"I guess I do. Finding the right girl is the secret, isn't it? Now, you're clear about tomorrow?"

It was the third time he'd asked me, and the morning

was young. I recited it again: "The two o'clock train and I'll bring the car back into the city."

"You have a set of keys?"

I nodded.

He moved around to the driver's side and stood there, looking at the brownstones that lined the street, then up at the sky, breathing deeply. "At least I'll be out of range for the fallout of whatever Mother gets up to. I'm not sorry to miss that."

I waited.

"You'd think I was putting off leaving."

I was thinking just that.

"Well, no man wants to get married. Good luck to you too, Gregor. Let me know if there's ever anything I can do for you. You've got the recommendation?"

I did.

"And Mackey's office will answer any further questions if anyone has any. I've told him, unconditional raves."

"Thank you, sir." I was ready to have him drive away.

"You have Mackey's number?"

I did.

He got into the car and put on dark glasses. He looked across at me. "You did pack the marriage license?"

"It's in the case with your passport, sir."

"You'd think I was nervous. Oh well, marriage is probably like what they say about murder, the first one's the hardest."

"I wouldn't know, sir," I told him. "I've never murdered anyone."

Mr. Theo laughed and turned on the motor. The street was temporarily untraveled, so he pulled out and was at last gone.

32

I MEET THE BEAR LADY

I was one of the first at the church. Mr. Wycliffe seated me, at my request, on the aisle at the rear of the groom's side. He looked darkly handsome, youthfully handsome, romantically handsome. "She still hasn't said a word," he reported to me.

"Sir?"

"About the baby. Why hasn't she told me?"

I couldn't have said. The organ played restrained Bach. Gradually at first, then in a rush, the church filled, until the scent of flowers fell back before the perfumes and colognes of the guests, and cut stones battled with stained glass to capture the eye.

On his way by my pew, seating the last arrivals, Mr. Wycliffe leaned over to tell me, "Now she wants to spend a month on Lake George. She even has a house there. I don't know why she thinks it'll be so easy for me to get away from the office for a month. On short notice."

"But you will be able to?"

He nodded. "She's up to something. I don't know... God, life gets complicated, loving someone, wanting her to be happy. Look—there he comes, there they are." He hurried away.

A minister, arrayed in his nuptial vestments, holding his prayer book before him, now waited at the front of the church. Mr. Theo and his brother, both in tails, came out to stand by the minister. They looked over the quieting congregation. The organ switched to Mendelssohn. From the distance, the men looked like three puppets, without individual character. They looked like animated costumes. Mr. Theo stiffened, in alarm I thought.

Turning my head, I saw that a woman had entered the church, as if it were for her that the processional pealed. She was a ripe blonde, who seemed to invest with sensuality even the innocent act of speaking her request into the ear of the usher. Her timing was remarkably bad.

I raised my hand, to indicate the empty seats next to me. The usher hustled her over and she sat down quickly, her cheeks flushed as if she were embarrassed, or had had to rush to make the occasion. "Thanks, friend," the familiar husky voice said. "This place is hard to locate. They say," she said, "small towns are easy to find your way around in, but you can't prove it by me." Then she moved a little away from me and sat back, upright in the stiff pew, dressed in dark blue with lace at her throat and wrists and a single pearl in her ear. Her hair tumbled in curls down her back.

The usher returned from seating Mrs. Rawling. The

music rose to a crescendo. We all stood up. The ceremony had begun.

I watched it out until we all rose again, at its conclusion. Mr. Theo, with Alexis on his arm, returned her down the aisle, married. Alexis wore yards of white satin and yards of lace. Her porcelain skin glowed. Her smile seemed genuine. She didn't look for me. She stepped serenely into her future and I wished her well.

The woman beside me was fumbling in her purse, so I gave her my handkerchief. She mopped at her eyes, as bridesmaids and ushers swept down the center aisle, two by two while glad music played. She blew her nose.

The front pews poured forth family.

"I always cry at weddings," the woman said. "That's that, I guess. She's no beauty, is she? Fantastic skin, though. She'll be good for him, you can tell. Do you happen to know, is there a back exit from this place?"

"Of course," I said. "Let me show you."

We slipped into the side aisle and back toward the altar, against the flow of traffic. On the street, a limousine was pulling away, with others lined up to follow, once they were filled. We took a shady path around to the parking lot.

"Here's your hanky," she said. "And thanks."

I didn't know if she was as much at a loss as she seemed. "I don't know where you're going now...?"

"Back to the city, if I can find the train station again, whenever the next train is."

"I'm driving into the city," I told her. "I'm leaving now, and if you like I could take you."

Her smile for me had sympathy in it. "So you weren't invited to the reception either? I wasn't exactly invited to the wedding, truth to tell, but you're allowed to, aren't you? I always heard anyone could go to the wedding, in the church. But anyway"—she stopped walking—"thanks, but I don't think I should—" She stopped speaking and shook her head at herself. "Who am I trying to kid?" she asked me. "You must be OK, you're the friend of a friend, right? Besides, this is the country, not like the big bad city. I'd be glad of a ride, truth to tell. It would be a help. Otherwise I'll just sit in the station and wish I was someplace else."

We moved on toward the car. I unlocked the door for her and opened it, but she had drawn back. "Wait a minute. This is Teddy's car. Isn't it?"

I gave her time to work it out.

"What are you doing with Teddy's car? Who are—? Wait a minute, wait a minute here. I thought you sounded familiar. You're the butler, aren't you. Are you the butler?"

She got into the car and leaned across to unlock my door. "Aren't you? On the phone?"

"Yes," I said.

"This is funny, this is really funny. You know who I am?"

"You have a distinctive voice," I told her. "An attractive voice, if I may say so."

"You certainly can say so." She was smiling as I started the motor, but it faded as we pulled out of the parking lot, leaving the church and the milling guests behind.

"So here we are, the butler and the mistress," she said. "What's your name?"

"Gregor."

"So, Gregor, here we are. How does a drink sound to you? I could use a drink, after that. I don't know why I thought I had to go, but I did. So I did. And that's that. A drink, and a little consolation, that's what I'd like. You're awfully good-looking for a butler."

I liked her, I have to admit it. "A drink sounds tempting," I told her, "but I should warn you, I seem to have temporarily given up sex."

"I may do that myself, Gregor. What we'll do is, we'll drink to Teddy. Can I have that hanky again?"

I passed it to her.

She sniffled beside me.

The road led us on.

"I should have known better than to come, but truth to tell? I love him. We've been pretty steady now for over a year. It'll be two years in the fall since we got introduced, and we always had a good time. Never once not, which is something, isn't it. It's not as if I thought he'd ever marry me. I'm not that stupid. I never thought that, and it's not as if he's the only guy around, either. It's just—I *know* him."

She blew her nose.

"I guess you're bound to end up loving someone, sooner or later. But I never kidded myself," she said, resolve in her voice. "And I won't start now. All the money in the world wouldn't give me what she's got."

I had stopped at an intersection and looked over at her. She was a strikingly attractive woman, long-legged, with a wide, full mouth. She wore her sensuality as unselfconsciously as a pansy bears its broad, velvety flowers. "Not looks," she answered my thoughts. "I'm much prettier, I know that. And sexier." She went on, trying to make me understand. "Even in that doll's dress—Do you know how much a dress like that costs? It'd make you cry, Gregor,

CYNTHIA VOIGT

honest it would. But she's no dolly, she's…So I guess I'd better just start to forget him."

How, I wondered, did Theodore Mondleigh manage to get these women? What was it he had? Money, I answered myself, and it was a bitter thought.

"Trouble is, Gregor, a guy like Teddy, I can't forget him." Her laugh was without rancor. "He thinks it's just sex, you know? He's a real babe in the woods."

228

33

HOPE ABANDONED

I'm a rational man. I know that worms have eaten men, and why—and also why not. I'm not without experience of women, of life, of what feels like—although it is not and never was—heartbreak. Grief and hope go together, like stocks and bonds. I almost hoped that Theodore Mondleigh would be a complete turn-off for her, that the chemistry would be all wrong, that their pheromones would jangle.

I had invested everything in my personal self, and it hadn't been enough.

But there is always plenty to do. I went to movies, plays, concerts, readings, museums, and galleries. I read *Barron's* with my morning coffee and altered some investments. In the evenings, after I had eaten and cleaned up, I went back upstairs to my rooms. My living area had a large plate-glass window, a double-glazed trapezoid that opened out to both a skyscape and a cityscape. Sometimes, under the tangential fall of sunlight at evening, it seemed that I looked out to a Renaissance city of towers and curved windows and stones as warm as flesh. I filled my rooms with music, the ordered inevitability of the *Brandenburg Concertos* for preference; I sat in a chair and divided my interest between *Bleak House* and the black buildings before me, pricked, like the night-time sky, with light.

And of course I thought. You make a decision, then one road leads to another, way leads on to way, until you find yourself in some dark, pathless forest, when all the time you thought you were on your way home. I understood that.

And how what *has* happened apotheosizes into fate. The past is fatal, the future has possibility.

It was time for a change. I thought of the Southwest, with its vast barren spaces. I thought of the high-headed Rockies. I thought of New Zealand's breathtaking geography.

I considered my financial position: I had invested and had an income a man could live off in comfort, if not splendor. Or a woman. I had a wardrobe that was likely to last a lifetime. A gentleman of independent means, I could be that.

I considered myself: school, a BA first, and then perhaps—I looked around my room—architecture, or interior design. There was museum curatorial work, which would require further degrees. Or I could return to my family.

They were alive and well, I knew that. I was alive and well, they knew that. I thought they would, with reason, be satisfied with my success. I wouldn't have to stay there, I could just return, to mark the adventure's end.

Meanwhile, I followed routines. I set the answering machine every day. "You have reached the Mondleigh residence. Please leave your name and number. A happy Bloomsday to you."

There was no message. I wasn't surprised.

"...on the anniversary of Victoria's accession to the throne."

Whirr, beep. "This is Alfred Jones at Domestic Services, Mr. Rostov. As I told you, we don't ordinarily list overseas positions, but I have made some inquiries for you. There is an opening for a caretaker in New Zealand. I must tell you, however, that the owner is a man of dubious reputation. Let me urge you to reconsider. With your experience and recommendations I could place you next month in Hawaii, Chicago, Phoenix, Pittsburgh, or Boston. All of these are suitable positions for you, with generous salaries. I hope you will reconsider before our appointment next week." *Beep, beep, beep.*

"A happy Walpurgis Night to you."

Beep. "Dr. Bernham's office calling, to remind Mr. Rostov of his appointment tomorrow, three p.m., for a cleaning." *Beep.*

Whirr, beep. "Mr. Rostov, Mrs. Wallace at Ludovic's calling. That's two tickets you haven't picked up. You must consider, Mr. Rostov, that others might have wanted them. Many people decide at the last minute, especially if they need only one seat. And it's more than three weeks since Walpurgis Night, Mr. Rostov. I hope all is well with you?" *Beep, beep, beep.*

"...on the anniversary of Kafka's birth."

Silence.

I went out, I came in, I ate and slept, I made my decisions and laid my plans, I changed my mind and my plans. The only fireworks I saw were those that made their lonely way up into the sky above the horizon of buildings outside my window on Independence Day. It seemed to me that I didn't know myself and that I might never have. It seemed to me that I had let myself make a terrible mistake.

34

ALEXIS RAWLING MONDLEIGH

A woman seated on the stoop of an Upper East Side New York City townhouse could be anyone. She could be anyone dressed in a long terra-cotta skirt and forest-green blouse, her brown hair held back by a broad ribbon of the same colors, her round arms bare and tanned and her face cupped in her hands, as if she were tired after a long journey. Suitcases waited by the door, a pair of them.

Alexis looked up. She stood up, smoothing her skirt. She didn't smile. "Gregor. You're here. I thought…"

"I thought for a minute you were Miss Sarah," I admitted, and took a deep breath. "You look well, Alexis."

She didn't answer.

"Very Italian," I said. Then I came to my senses. "I didn't expect you back until—"

"Aren't you going to let me in?" she interrupted.

"Of course, I'm sorry. You must be tired. I'm almost packed; I can be out in under an hour. I'm sorry, Alexis," I said. I took the house key out of my pocket and gave it to her, so I could pick up the suitcases. I handed her the little sack of toiletries I had been out to purchase. She didn't move. I stood holding the suitcases. "If you'll get the door?" I asked her.

She unlocked the doors and held them for me. I put the suitcases down at the foot of the stairs and went along to the kitchen. There were just the breakfast dishes to be washed, just an overnight bag to be packed. I had reserved a room at the Gramercy Park Hotel. I should have left a day earlier: I'd known I was just staying on.

"Gregor." She had followed me.

"I'll be just a minute here, Miss—Mrs.—"

I felt stupid. I'd been stupid. I was caught out in my own stupidity.

"Gregor, stop that."

I turned off the water.

"Look at me."

I looked at her, ashamed.

"I've left him. Theo. In Paris."

She waited.

"Did you hear me?"

"I think so," I said. "Maybe you should repeat it?"

"I've left my husband, left Theo. He's in Paris. Or that's where he was last night."

"Why?"

It wasn't what she expected me to say, but I had to be careful not to presume. I don't know what she saw, watching me the way she did.

"I've got to admit, I hoped I'd find you...oh, drunk and unshaven, or something."

I was sorry to disappoint her. "I gave myself two weeks."

"It's been four."

"Almost five."

I didn't know what to say. There was no reason to presume she had come back for me. To me.

"Two weeks until what?" she asked cautiously.

"Alexis, just let me get these dishes into the dishwasher, and I'll pour coffee—and—" And what? I didn't know. I just knew I'd be better able to deal with it over a cup of coffee. I was afraid, of course.

"You aren't making this easy for me, Gregor."

"I'm sorry," I said sincerely.

"Or are you trying to make it easy? To let me down easy?"

I bent to pull out a tray. "No," I said. "But this is his house. His kitchen. You're his wife. It doesn't seem right—"

She thought for a moment. "All right, I can see that. I understand. Should I take my suitcases up to your room?"

"No."

I didn't know what to say, I didn't know what to do. Everything I said came out sounding like what I didn't mean. I made up a tray and she followed me up the back stairs, carrying the coffeepot.

I put the tray down on the writing table. My own suitcases stood ready by the door. She set the pot down and went to stand by the big window but didn't look out. She looked around the room. "This is really nice, Gregor, and big too."

I poured out two cups of coffee.

"You've got the best view in the house, don't you?"

"Mr. Mondleigh is a good employer."

Her blouse fell softly from her shoulders, and the skirt hung in gentle folds. The effect was plump and delicious, like a peach. The window framed her, so that the sky began at her shoulders.

"Theo was angry," she said. I gave her a coffee cup. I didn't sit down either. "At me. Thanks. Humiliated too, of course."

"What did you tell him?"

"I told him—Well, first, that it wasn't going to work. I thought that was pretty clear, because it was clear to me and I don't know anything. There's a lot more to love than sex. I know, it's a cliché."

"The cliché might be an underrated manner of speech."

She was too involved in what she wanted to say to mock me. "And I didn't *want* to love him, to be able to love him. That's what I wanted, to *not* be able to. I didn't give him a chance. Poor Theo, and yes, I'm ashamed of myself. But I did tell him about you when he asked me why. He said things were going great, and maybe he thought they were, maybe he didn't know? So I told him there was someone else." She challenged me, "I could have done it, you know; I could have stayed with Theo."

"That's what I was afraid of," I said.

"Why were you afraid?"

"Because—you know, he's not a bad man. In fact—"

"And he was trying. Whenever we weren't doing anything, a museum, or seeing a sight, nothing scheduled—if there was any danger we might have to talk, I think—he'd send me shopping. And everything kept reminding me of you."

"We never went shopping," I reminded her.

"And the sex—You know, Gregor? It's always sex, always the same. But, Gregor? I didn't know you loved me, until Theo made love to me."

I didn't want to hear about it.

"You didn't *tell* me," she said. "Why didn't you? You shouldn't have just let me be so stupid. I am so sorry, Gregor."

I didn't know what to say.

"I should have known right away. And I guess I did. I should have told him right away, but…That's why it took me so long. Did it take me too long? Are you sorry to see me, Gregor?" she demanded. "What is it? You can tell me the truth. You owe me that."

"Sorry?" I set my coffee cup down; it was rattling in its saucer.

"Well, you haven't…or anything."

Not because I hadn't felt like it. Not because I hadn't wanted to. "Alexis, what I'm feeling—I could explode, spontaneously combust, like in Dickens. All this time, I didn't know if you had any idea. Or if you had any idea, if you'd *do* anything. Have the nerve to, be foolhardy enough to—You are such a mystery to me, I never know."

She needed it clearer. "Then you aren't angry?"

"Not angry. Not displeased. After knowing every minute of every one of these long days how different it would be if you were with me? Really there, here, present, not just remembered. Or imagined."

"That's almost as good as drunk and unshaven," Alexis

said, her voice shaky but her eyes, under that Renaissance forehead, shining.

"We aim to please."

She was still puzzled, and she had every right to be. But I wanted no danger that later either one of us would think that I had taken advantage of her.

"Does Mr. Theo know—?"

"Who you are? Yes. He needed to be convinced; he didn't just believe me. Then he said—Well, in essence he said I was letting myself be taken advantage of."

"Taken in," I revised.

"Because I don't know anything about you, he said." She was speaking as carefully as I was, now.

"And you said?"

"What could I say? I don't, I don't know anything about you, not the way he meant it. And I love you."

I jammed my hands into my pockets and locked my kneecaps. "Will you get a divorce?"

"Oh yes. There'll be no difficulty about that."

"Will you marry me?"

It was the question. I couldn't put it more clearly.

"You mean, marry you on your terms. You mean keeping my money. Putting it in both our names." She took a breath and admitted reluctantly, "I don't like it, Gregor."

"For what it's worth, I do entirely love you." The plain truth.

"Oh," she said. "Oh." And smiled, as if she had as much riding on this as I did. "That's all right then. But Gregor?"

Her tone of voice warned me.

"I want to live *your* real life too. First. For a while, a year or two. And I mean the really real one, not this sham."

238

"This sham?"

"Pretending you aren't what you are, as if you were ashamed."

I'd never thought I might be ashamed, but when I thought of it, I could have laughed. It never does to underestimate an intelligent woman. And for all her compliance and kindness, generosity, and courage too, the woman was above all intelligent.

"We could hire out as a couple," she suggested.

"You can't do that. What can you do?"

"Don't underestimate me, Gregor." I'd made her angry.

"It would be a waste. Of your education, your mind, your abilities."

"No more than yours," she countered. "Just so that we can start out really together," she said.

"You mean," I worked it out, "starting out equal."

"Will you?"

I wasn't the only one allowed to make terms. I played for time. "Those colors, that outfit—"

"Do you like it? It's sort of Etruscan, I thought."

"I was thinking Renaissance, but you're right."

"And flattering," she said, without vanity.

"Very flattering. You look...not naked but...the way you look, naked." I didn't know who I thought I was kidding, hesitating like that. "All right, Alexis. I think you're probably right."

"About what?"

"No more sham life. The real one, for the two of us."

She put down her coffee cup. "For a romantic, who's been proposed to twice, I have to say it's been a disappointing experience."

"Has it?" I was giddy with it all, as if I had just won Wimbledon a second before, just played the winning point, and was just beginning to comprehend my victory. "Then"—and I fell onto my knees before her, in the time-honored tradition—"Alexis, dear heart, I've been helplessly in love with you since I first saw you, reeling down Sixty-Second Street, quite drunk—"

"I was not," she protested. "Tipsy but not—And you didn't, either." But she was laughing too now. "I'd better take what I can get. Get up, Gregor, and—"

I had her in my arms before she could say any more, and she had me in her arms. Memory and imagination, even the poignancy of dreams, they are nothing like the flesh itself. Reality is the most poignant dream.

At the end of the long, satisfying kiss, "Yes," I said. "Now, we'd better get going."

"All right." She wasn't even surprised. She didn't move out of my arms.

"I'll finish packing, we'll rinse out the coffeepot, get these cups into the dishwasher. We have to see your parents of course."

"We?"

"We," I told her, firmly. I stayed within her arms, looking down at her face.

"They're in Connecticut."

I laid it out patiently, probably grinning like a fool. I felt like grinning. "We'll take a cab, rent a car, then drive out to see your parents. In Connecticut."

"They might not be too pleased," she said.

"I'm prepared to like them, Alexis, because they're

your parents. But I don't think their disapproval would cast much of a pall on my day."

Alexis loaded the dishwasher while I put a message on the machine. "You have reached the Mondleigh residence. If you will leave your name and number, your call will be returned." Alexis held the doors while I carried our suitcases down to the street. The phone rang. I was occupied punching the code into the electronic alarm and didn't answer it. Out in the street, Alexis had found a cab. She and the cabbie were loading suitcases into the trunk. I hesitated just inside the door.

"I don't understand, Mr. Bear," the familiar voice said. It came down the hallway as if the woman herself were in the kitchen, speaking. "Does it mean you're coming back? I don't need a Paris nightgown, you silly bear, you know I don't. Just call me, whenever. I'll be here."

35

REALITY

It wasn't until I took the exit from the Merritt onto the Hutchinson River Parkway that she asked, "They didn't really mind. Do you think?"

"They were too shocked to know what they thought."

"Until you told my father why you looked familiar to him."

"He'll adjust," I promised her. "We're just an old story, the heiress and the chauffeur."

"Don't be cynical at me, Gregor."

"That wasn't cynicism. It was nerves," I admitted.

"Really?" She turned her head to look at me. I kept my eyes on the narrow roadway, the trees rushing by and winding curves and late-morning traffic hurtling toward the city. "You didn't seem nervous. You never seem nervous."

"We are none of us what we seem," I warned her.

"What do you have to be nervous about now?"

I could have told her, but I didn't. Because until you've claimed your prize, you don't even understand how much you have to lose. If I'd told her.

We were across the Tappan Zee and I had failed to take the Palisades Parkway exit before she spoke again. "Where are you going?"

"Home."

"Pittsburgh," she said. Well, she was right, or near enough. "I thought—You said you'd left home. If it's been fifteen years…"

"I never had anything to go home to before."

"And now you do?"

"Now I do. You."

"That doesn't make sense."

"Yes it does."

"I don't understand you," she said.

"Do you mind?"

"No, but don't you?"

"You know," I said, signaling and then turning off onto the Garden State, "it's asking an awful lot, asking to be understood. As if it weren't enough to be loved."

I'd silenced her again. I didn't try to talk.

Eventually, we entered the Jersey Turnpike. I passed her the ticket and she stuck it into the visor over her head without a word, as if we were an old married couple. "All right," she said. "The money is a problem," she began.

I didn't argue. No money is a problem, lots of money is a problem, and anything in between is a problem.

"I want to use it for…useful things. There are plenty of good causes, making loans to start small businesses, to women and blacks and Hispanics—people banks won't loan to. Employing the homeless—there are all kinds of ideas out there—and the arts too. Not all of it, and not an absolute gift, but the income…Gregor, you don't know how much there is. Or do you?"

"How would I?"

"You could look it up. You didn't, did you?"

"No, I took you on appearances."

"But can I? I mean, can we?"

"How much of it do you want to give away?"

"Use. I said *use*," she said.

"Not the exact number, just percentages."

"I thought, maybe half."

"Would that be enough to establish a trust?"

"A foundation, you mean?" She thought. "A minor one, maybe."

I considered this. "Before or after taxes?" I asked. "Half before or after taxes?"

She started to laugh. "I haven't thought it out; I'm not in a good position to negotiate details. It's not easy to use money well."

"If we did start a foundation, that could be your work," I offered her.

"Work?" She thought about it. "Yes, it would be, it could, couldn't it? I think I like that, Gregor. Gregor? I am so glad—"

"So am I, Alexis," I promised her. "So am I. Have you thought about prisons?" I asked.

"I don't think it's possible to establish private prisons, Gregor. They're not like libraries."

"I mean, a study of penal systems. Because jails are not

only terrible places, they're also ineffective, which may be the worst thing about them."

"You haven't been to jail, have you?"

"I told you I wasn't a criminal."

"I know. I remember. But I think you were always very careful about what you said."

"Very careful," I agreed.

From Trenton to King of Prussia I had doubts and anxieties. Alexis, I thought, had doubts and fears. I didn't blame either one of us.

"Anyway," I heard myself say, "you can't get married until you get divorced, so you've got time to change your mind."

"I don't usually change my mind," she said. I waited, giving her the chance. "I'll marry you today, if you want."

"That's bigamy," I protested.

"That depends," Alexis said, "on whether you choose the starry law without or the moral law within."

"That's Kant," I protested again, and I laughed.

"I do love you, Gregor Rostov," she promised me.

I didn't doubt her. She loved Gregor Rostov, no question. But what about me? Did she love me? And if so, did she love me enough?

Cozying up to your anxieties gets you nowhere, so I opted for wallowing in the gladness, which, if temporary, was at least present. "When?" I asked her. "Since when?"

"Since the first, maybe. But that could be hindsight. Certainly since the second or third. It wasn't that I didn't know," she explained, "but I thought there was nothing I could do. I thought it was just one of those things that was too bad. True, and too bad, but I would go on with my life."

"From the first?"

"You looked so…"

Eligible, was my most cynical expectation. *Handsome*, maybe, *attractive, exciting, mysterious.*

"…as if you were looking for a friend. And you talked to me. We talked."

"I roused your maternal instincts?"

"Not maternal. Don't play dumb. What about you?"

"What about me what?"

"When did you?"

"You're not going to like it."

"How do you know?"

"In Pittsburgh," I said. "When we…" There was no word adequate to that occasion; the word hasn't yet been written that incorporates the physical, emotional, and metaphysical. The first two, maybe, but nothing touches on the metaphysical aspect of sex, and unless it does, it doesn't do the job. "In Pittsburgh. Before, I knew how much I liked you, but I didn't know I loved you."

"And they say women are hopeless romantics."

"Who says? It's men who say that, in their canons of literature, men and the male critics who explicate them. What do they know?"

By the time we stopped to eat hamburgers just east of Harrisburg, we were both too deeply immersed in a discussion of the place of women in the arts to worry about who paid for lunch or for gas. Alexis drove the last long section of the Turnpike. I directed her to get off at the Perry Valley exit and then go south on Route 19. She looked at the fast-food restaurants, gas stations, motels, and malls crowding around the stoplighted intersections, obscuring the long summer twilight. "What's going to happen now? I don't want to spend the night alone in some sleazy motel," she told me, apologizing.

"What about with me? With me in some sleazy motel?"

"That would be OK. If your family—if your parents—I can stay in Pittsburgh, I'd be all right alone where we stayed before."

"We'll see how it goes," I told her. "Here, turn here, onto seventy-nine. It's only a few miles, maybe ten." Seventy-nine had been built since my time, but I'd looked at the map and knew which exit we wanted. Once we were off seventy-nine, the back roads were familiar but Alexis drove them warily, as they wound up and around the hills of western Pennsylvania. The gateway we turned at surprised her—I was watching her face—and the long driveway climbing up the slope of the hill, the respectably aged trees and the well-tended green lawns. I could hear her mind ticking over, making connections, drawing conclusions. My mind had ceased functioning. I could only hope.

The driveway branched before it circled to the front entrance of the house, and I directed her around the west wing to the garage. We got out of the car into the hot, sullen air July brings to the Ohio River Valley. "Muggy, isn't it?" I remarked.

"I guess your parents work here," Alexis said, looking up at the house. "That makes sense. I'd just...expected something different, some context in which I had no experience. Something entirely unknown. It's going to be harder than I thought, Gregor. What did they do with four children? Your parents."

"It's a pretty big place," I told her.

I led her up flagstone steps to a broad patio that ran all along the back of the house. Some of the French doors stood open to the cooler evening air. Below the stone balustrade, grassy lawns fell away. A golden evening was just changing into purple twilight, and in the east wing dining room I could see a table set with candles. I went over to the balustrade and looked down to where the swimming pool, like a giant aquamarine, was partially visible. "If my guess is correct, they'll be—" I managed to say, before my throat closed up on me.

Two people sat at the poolside, dressed for dinner, suit and silk.

"I don't see them." She looked down at the seated couple, and the pool, poolhouse, gardens beyond. "Where—"

And then she saw it.

"What is your name. Really."

I took a breath. "Reikel. Gregory. Allen. Gregory Allen Reikel don't run away, Alexis."

"I don't."

"Don't turn away," I specified.

She turned back to face me.

"You lied to me."

"I never lied to you."

"A fake. Reikel Mining. I'm a stockholder."

"Will you let me explain?"

She wasn't interested in any explanation. "An important stockholder. You deliberately deceived me. What was it, some kind of test?"

"Maybe." I didn't dare reach for her hand. I didn't dare give her the chance for a definitive gesture. "But who was I testing?"

She was too intelligent not to see it. "But it was terrible, it is, what you've done to me, Gregor. Gregory."

"Any more terrible that what you did to me? No"—I put my hands up to ward off her response—"that's no argument. It *was* terrible, I can't deny, I won't deny it."

I would have liked to, to argue that since it brought us to love, everything had to be right. But everything had changed between us now. Always before, I'd known more than she had, about love, about myself—even about what she knew. Now things were equal, we stood equal, and it was up to her.

"You really played me for a fool." But the sharp, dismissive anger was gone from her voice.

"Just listen. Please. When I left home I was eighteen—eighteen, Alexis, that's so young. I don't have to tell you what my life was like, you've lived it. I was idealistic and… it made me angry, I don't know how to explain. Alexis? Listen. Remember the girl I told you about?"

"She got pregnant."

"I loved her. I thought we were the great love story of the Western world. And who knows? Maybe we would have been. But my father—he offered her money, for an abortion, a settlement too. He went to her house and offered it, and she took it. It wasn't even very much money, but she thought it was. For me, a price for me."

"Oh," Alexis said.

"I wanted to marry her. She knew I did, we'd talked

about it. I could have supported us without any help from my family and she knew that too, but she took the money."

"Oh," Alexis said.

"So I left home. I was angry."

"What about your parents?"

"I wasn't in any mood to compromise, and they...they'd been knocked pretty hard, between Lisa—my sister—and me. They let me go. I think, they thought I'd be right back, probably. My father said I was trying to live in some fairy-tale world."

What had seemed so right, what had seemed my only chance—I didn't know how to make Alexis see it. "They didn't think I really would, or could. It was like a dare—or a sneer. I was *young*. Remember eighteen?"

"So you did it to show them? Is that what I'm for?"

"To show me, Alexis. You're for me."

The house, silver in twilight, the candlelit table, the shining jewel of a pool: she looked around at all of them, and I was afraid of what she was thinking. But I had no idea what she was thinking. "My God, you've got courage," she said.

I didn't dare to interrupt her.

"And so do I, don't I?" she said, as if she hadn't known it. "All right," she said.

"I did lie to you. I meant you to misunderstand."

"I know," she said. "Just tell me one thing, Gregory Reikel," trying on the name. "Do you have any more surprises for me? Any more of these metamorphoses? These earthquake occasions?"

"Surprises, I hope. But nothing more like this. This is it. This is me."

"Your parents won't like it, my being married."

"They'll get entirely the wrong idea about you," I agreed.

"Mine, on the other hand—"

"Does that mean you will? Marry me? And—?"

"How can you even ask?"

I lost my cool, my dignity, composure, self-control, lost all pretense. "Just answer, please, just say yes. I know, but say it to me, to me myself."

"Yes," she said.

I moved along the patio, to the broad steps that led down. She came with me, without any hesitation. Then she laughed out loud, setting her foot on the last step. "That's quite some trust I'll be managing. Gregory. Allen. Reikel." And she laughed again.

"What do you mean?"

"I mean, what's mine is yours, as we agreed."

I nodded. I remembered.

"And what's yours is mine, as we agreed."

I nodded again, dumb with surprise.

"Which makes a tidy sum," she concluded.

I could have protested, but I'd have felt like a fool trying it. I'd agreed to equality, and reality. I'd even known they might be troubling, but I'd thought Alexis was the only one who'd be troubled by them. I had to laugh. "I like your attitude. 'Tidy sum' sounds much better than 'filthy rich.'"

"Half of our combined incomes will make a substantial foundation."

"Or a third," I suggested. "After taxes. Whatever, it'll keep you busy. Exercise your leadership abilities. Exercise your financial skills. You can work at home," I said, reaching out for her hand, "and not have to leave the children."

She clutched at my fingers. "What about children? We haven't talked about anything important yet, Gregor. Gregory. Children, and where do we live, and what you'll do—because you can't not work—and—"

"There's time," I told her. "We have plenty of time now."

She stopped dead. She dropped my hand and turned to face me, but standing back, away. Her eyes were cast down. "Gregory?"

Her voice was so little I could barely hear it. I couldn't answer her right away, however, because the last sunlight was brushing her skin and hair with golden shadows, and my breath was caught in my throat.

"There's something I have to tell you."

When she raised her face, to make herself say it, her eyes glistened. I had seen them glistening like that once before, the last time we made love. When we both knew it was the last time.

"Don't," I asked her.

She shook her head. "I have to. I'm ashamed, but I ought to tell you."

"Whatever it is, it's all right."

She shook her head again. "I'm relieved," she said, unsmiling. "I mean I'm"—her eyes glistened—"really relieved. Because I was afraid. Afraid for myself, not even for the two of us, only myself. And I'm so glad you're not—I'm so glad you're—" She couldn't finish. "I'm sorry, Gregory," she said, "I've lied all along, to myself, but you too. Didn't you ever wonder about that weekend? I did. After. I think I would have made up anything to get you in bed and I wouldn't even admit it to myself. How much does this change things for you?"

Women, I thought. What kind of perfection do they expect from themselves? And I said just that to her.

For a minute, I was afraid she was going to argue the question, but "I hope so," was all she answered.

I didn't know what she was thinking. I wondered what she was thinking.

"I should have known, shouldn't I?" she asked, as we moved along the gravel path. She was asking herself, not me, but I answered her anyway.

"Maybe you did. Maybe you saw right through me."

"We could believe that," she suggested.

"We could believe that," I agreed.

I let go of her hand and put my arm around her shoulders. Her arm went around me. We moved along the path in step, with her bare, round-boned shoulder under my hand and her fingers up under my suit jacket, her fingertips at my waist. The man saw us first. I watched him rise from his chair, with more hope than apprehension, or so it seemed to me. Perhaps because that's what I myself was feeling.

Cynthia Voigt won the Newbery Medal for *Dicey's Song* and the Newbery Honor Award for *A Solitary Blue*, both part of the beloved Tillerman Cycle. She is also the author of many other celebrated books for middle-grade and teen readers, including *Izzy, Willy-Nilly* and *Jackaroo*. She was awarded the Margaret A. Edwards Award in 1995 for her work in literature, and the Katahdin Award in 2004. She lives in Maine.